D0065091

The HAUNTED SURFBOARD

by Anthony Masters

ILLUSTRATED BY PETER DENNIS

Librarian Reviewer
Allyson A.W. Lyga MS
Library Media/Graphic Novel Consultant
Fulbright Memorial Fund Scholar, author

Reading Consultant
Elizabeth Stedem
Educator/Consultant, Colorado Springs, CO
MA in Elementary Education, University of Denver, CO

STONE ARCH BOOKS
Minneapolis   San Diego

First published in the United States in 2007
by Stone Arch Books,
151 Good Counsel Drive, P.O. Box 669,
Mankato, Minnesota 56002.
www.stonearchbooks.com

Originally published in Great Britain in 1999
by A & C Black Publishers Ltd,
38 Soho Square, London, W1D 3HB.

Text copyright © 1999 Anthony Masters
Illustrations copyright © 1999 Peter Dennis

Library of Congress Cataloging-in-Publication Data
Masters, Anthony.
   The Haunted Surfboard / by Anthony Masters; illustrated by Peter Dennis.
   p. cm. — (Graphic Quest)
   ISBN-13: 978-1-59889-080-8 (hardcover)
   ISBN-10: 1-59889-080-8 (hardcover)
   ISBN-13: 978-1-59889-215-4 (paperback)
   ISBN-10: 1-59889-215-0 (paperback)
   1. Graphic novels. I. Dennis, Peter, 1950– II. Title. III. Series.
PN6727.M246H38 2007
741.5'973—dc22   2006007257

Summary: The only good thing about Jack's new school is that it is near the ocean and
he loves to surf. Then Jack meets Peter Stafford, a daredevil surfer who insists on risking
his life every time he enters the water.

Art Director: Heather Kindseth
Colorist: Kathy Clobes
Graphic Designer: Brann Garvey
Production Artist: Keegan Gilbert

1 2 3 4 5 6 11 10 09 08 07 06

Printed in the United States of America.

TABLE OF CONTENTS

CHAPTER ONE

Jack Morton raced after his classmate, yelling furiously.

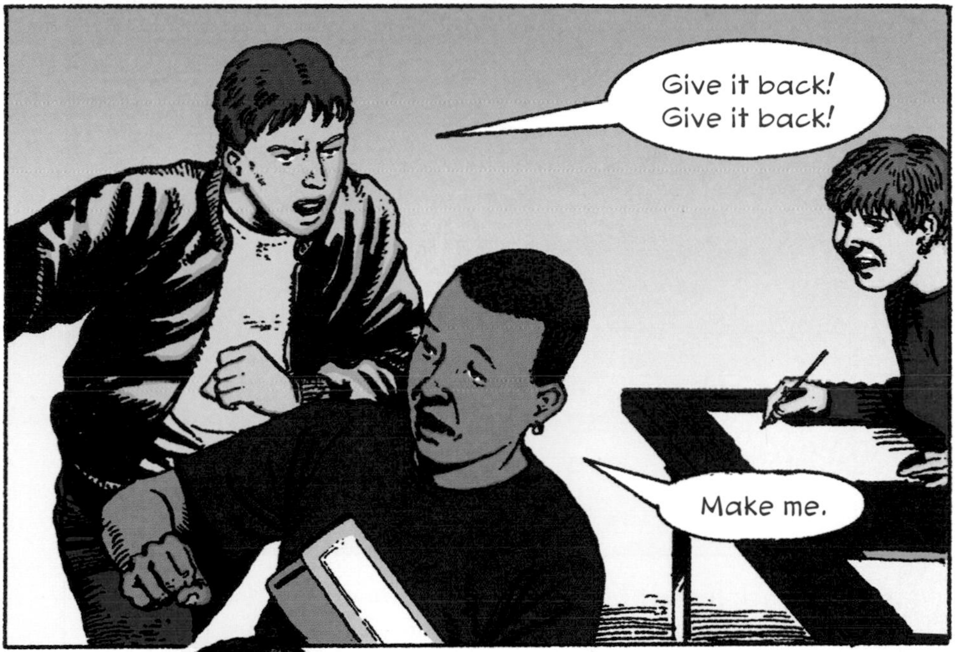
Give it back!
Give it back!
Make me.

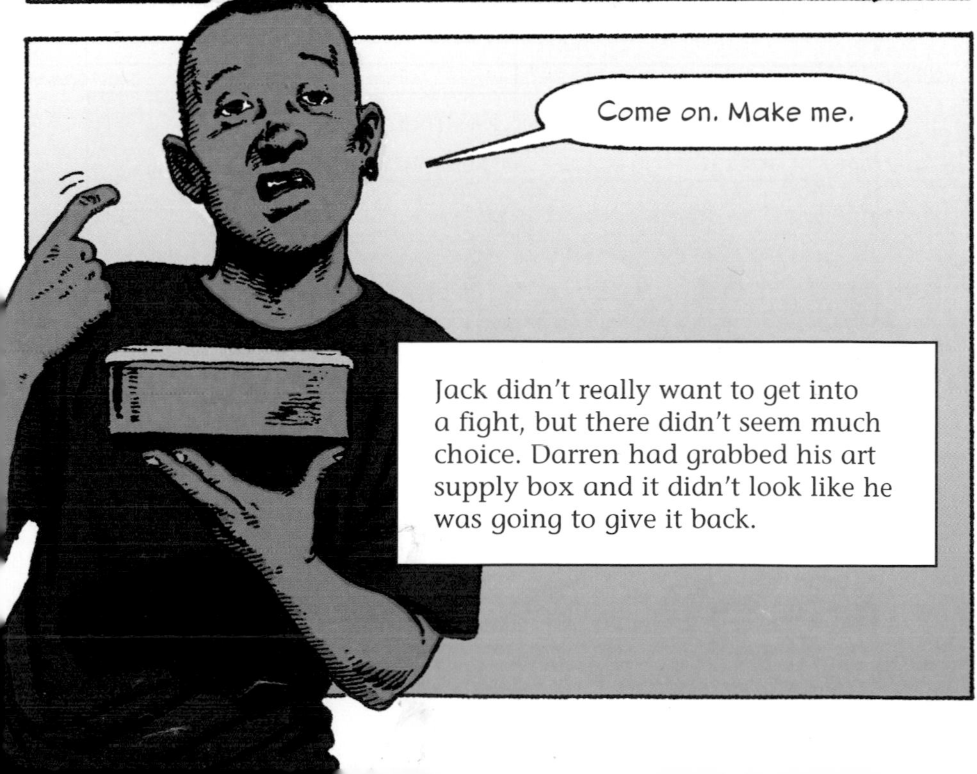
Come on. Make me.
Jack didn't really want to get into a fight, but there didn't seem much choice. Darren had grabbed his art supply box and it didn't look like he was going to give it back.

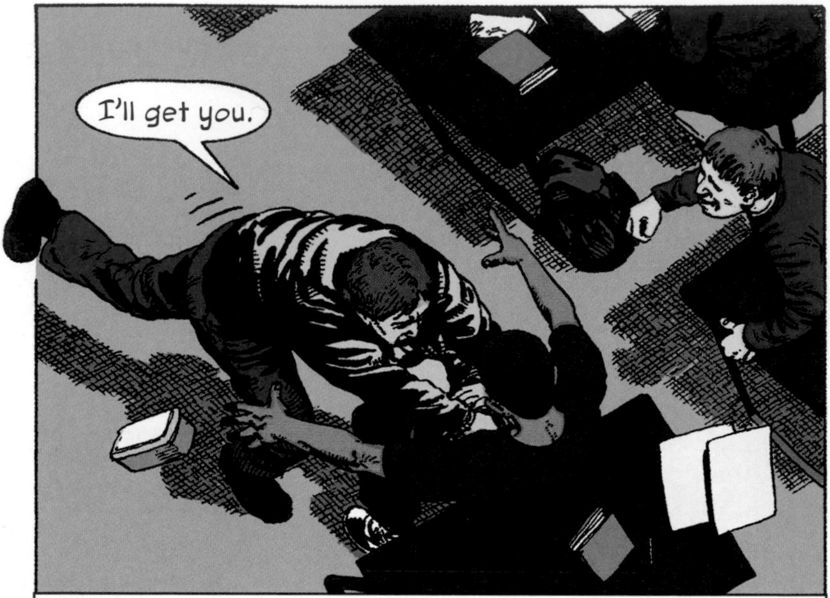
I'll get you.

Jack threw himself at Darren, knocking the box to the ground. As the two boys fought, they lost their balance, and were soon rolling around on the floor.

Mr. Dawkins, their teacher, was there in seconds.

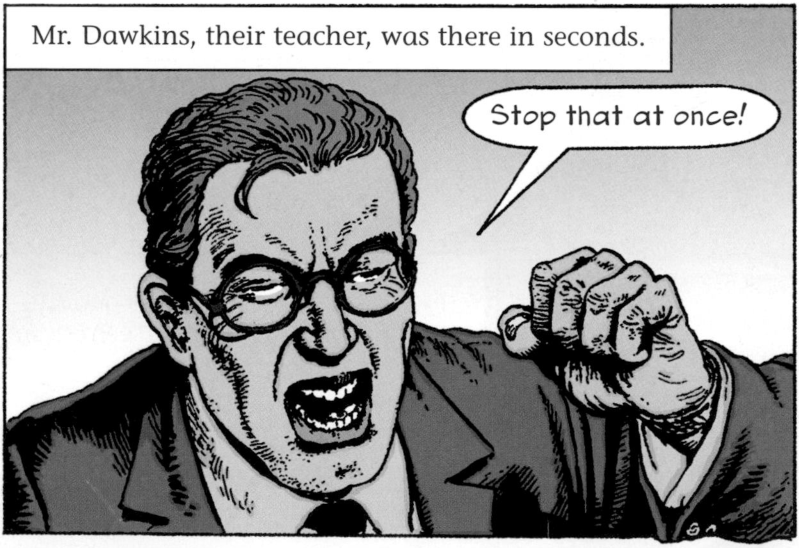
Stop that at once!

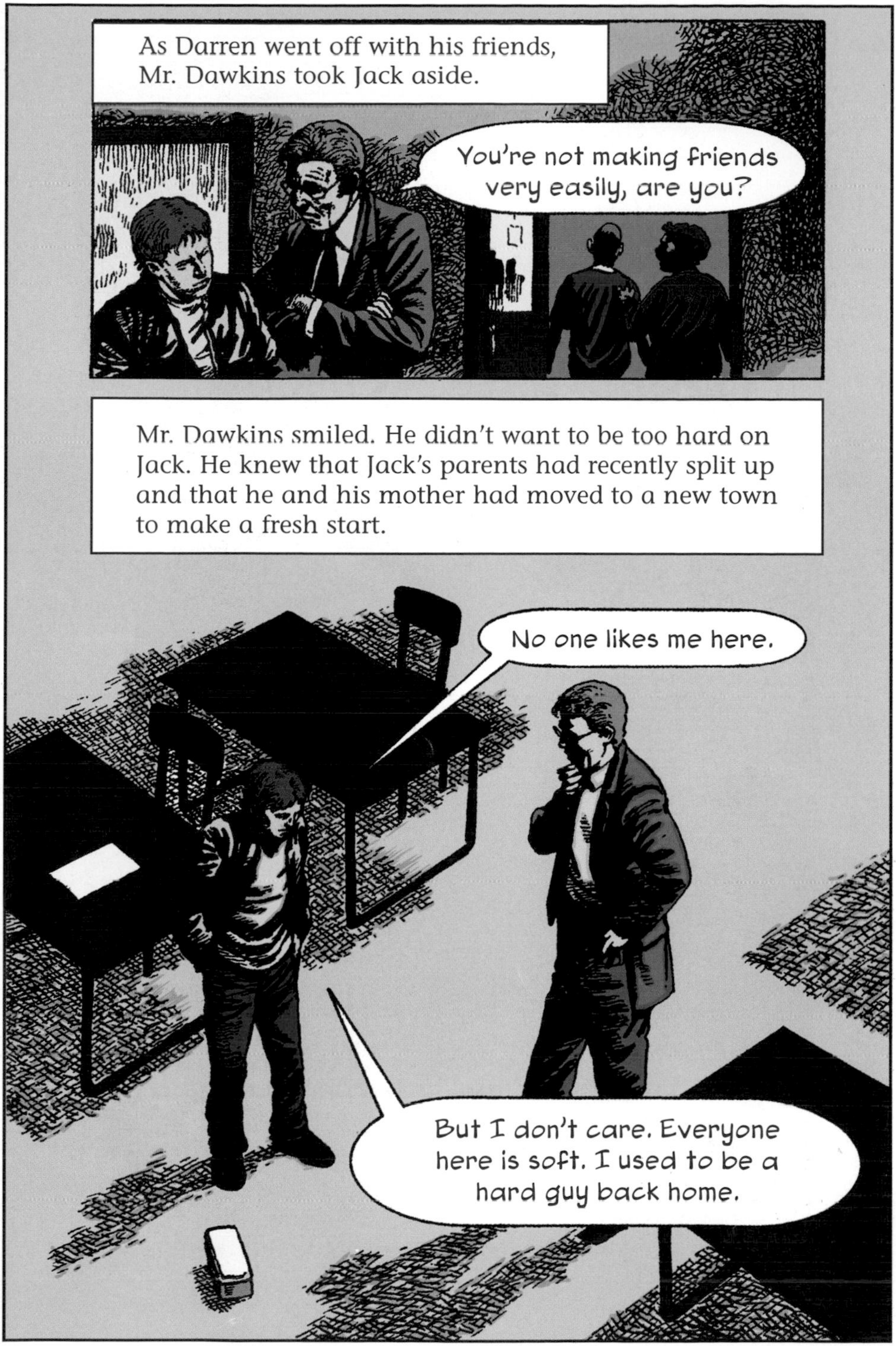
As Darren went off with his friends, Mr. Dawkins took Jack aside.
You're not making friends very easily, are you?
Mr. Dawkins smiled. He didn't want to be too hard on Jack. He knew that Jack's parents had recently split up and that he and his mother had moved to a new town to make a fresh start.
No one likes me here.
But I don't care. Everyone here is soft. I used to be a hard guy back home.

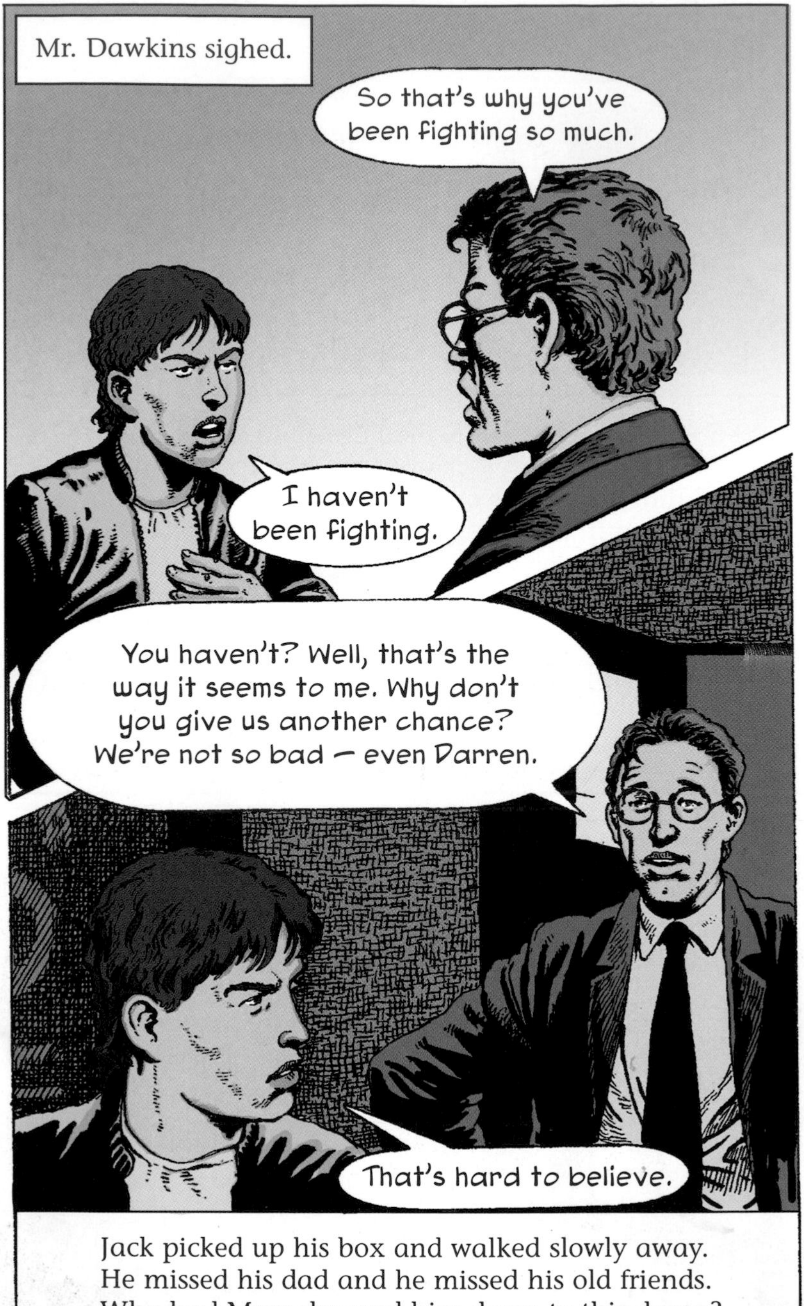
Mr. Dawkins sighed.
So that's why you've been fighting so much.
I haven't been fighting.
You haven't? Well, that's the way it seems to me. Why don't you give us another chance? We're not so bad — even Darren.
That's hard to believe.
Jack picked up his box and walked slowly away. He missed his dad and he missed his old friends. Why had Mom dragged him down to this dump?

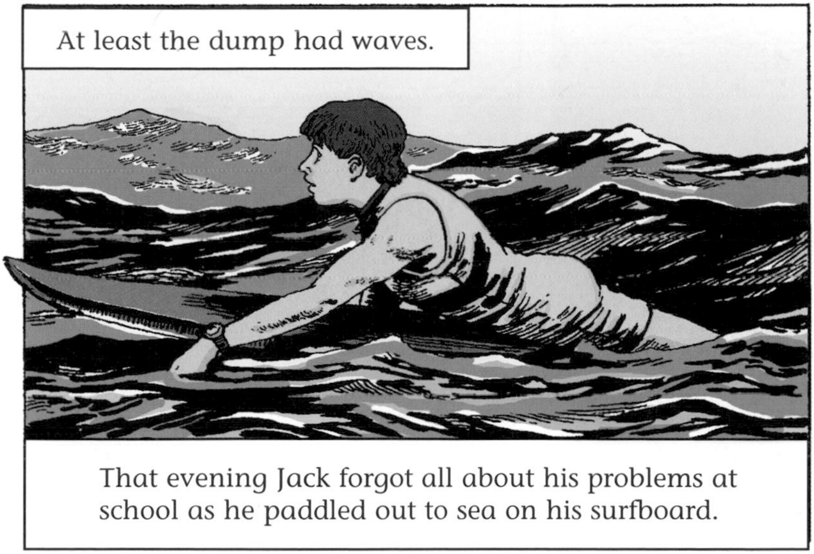
At least the dump had waves.
That evening Jack forgot all about his problems at school as he paddled out to sea on his surfboard.

There was no one else around and Jack was disappointed. He did want to make friends. Even if the other kids at school wouldn't accept him, surely the surfers would. But the beach was long and lonely and, as usual, deserted.

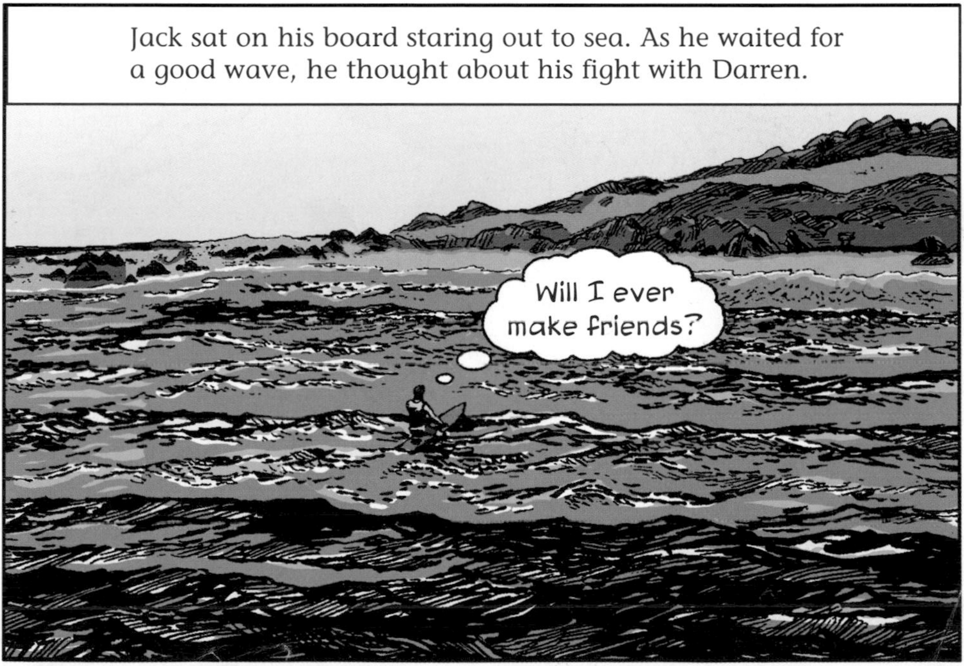
Jack sat on his board staring out to sea. As he waited for a good wave, he thought about his fight with Darren.
Will I ever make friends?

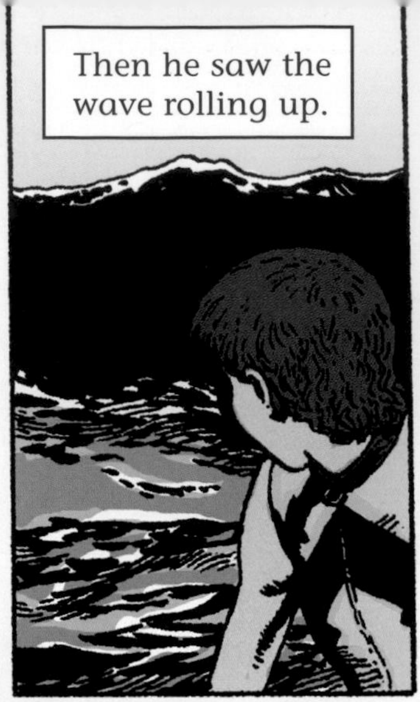
Then he saw the wave rolling up.

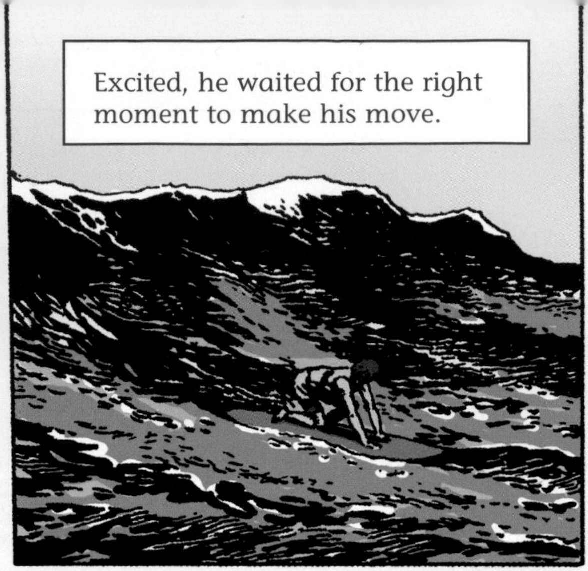
Excited, he waited for the right moment to make his move.

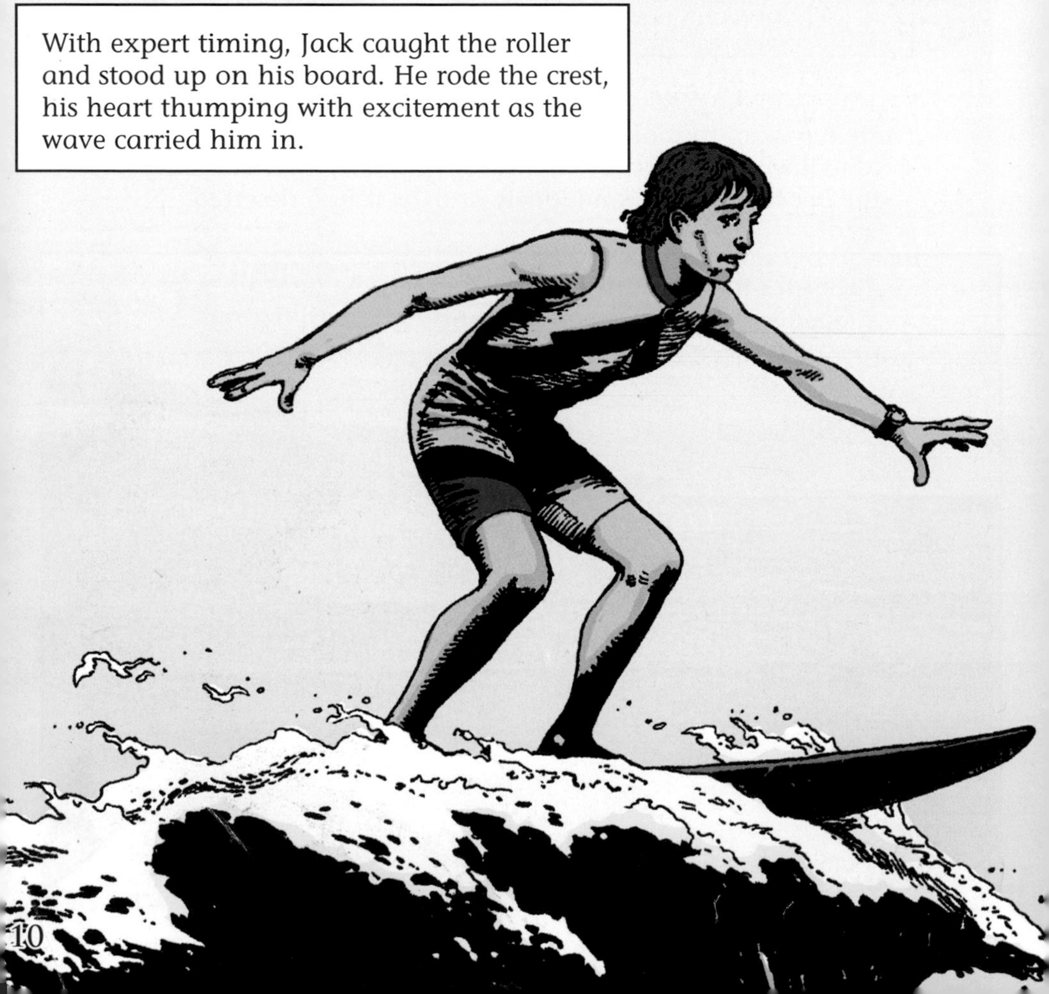
With expert timing, Jack caught the roller and stood up on his board. He rode the crest, his heart thumping with excitement as the wave carried him in.

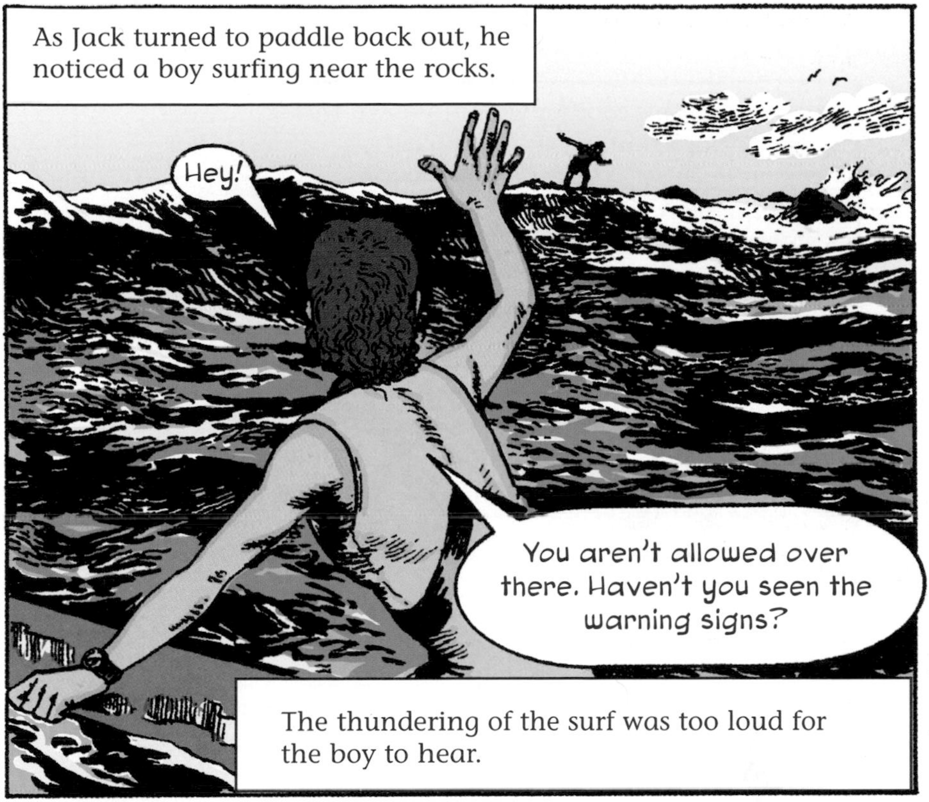
As Jack turned to paddle back out, he noticed a boy surfing near the rocks.
Hey!
You aren't allowed over there. Haven't you seen the warning signs?
The thundering of the surf was too loud for the boy to hear.

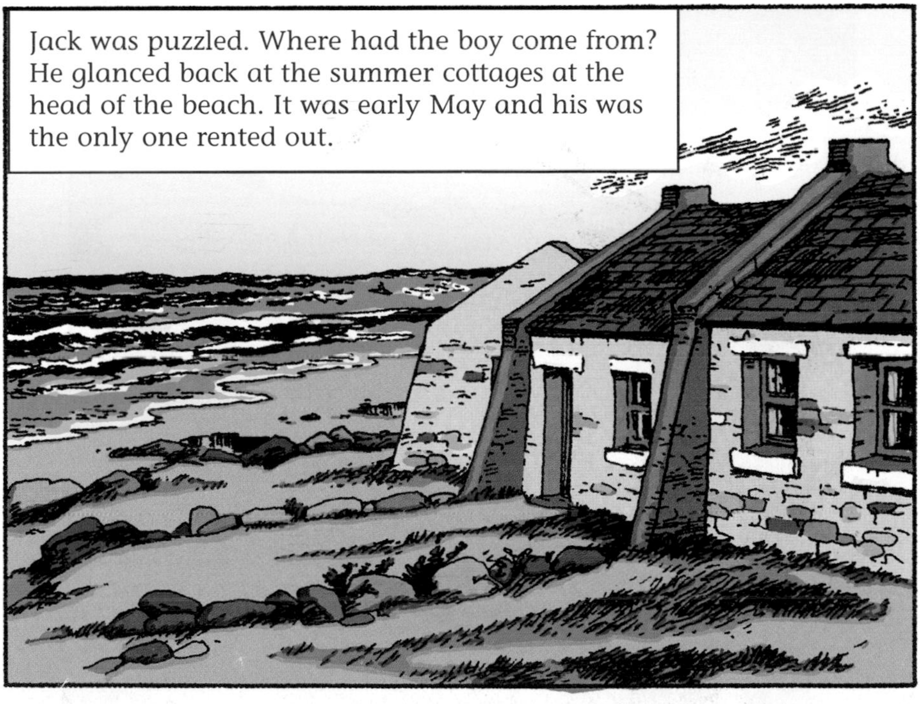
Jack was puzzled. Where had the boy come from? He glanced back at the summer cottages at the head of the beach. It was early May and his was the only one rented out.

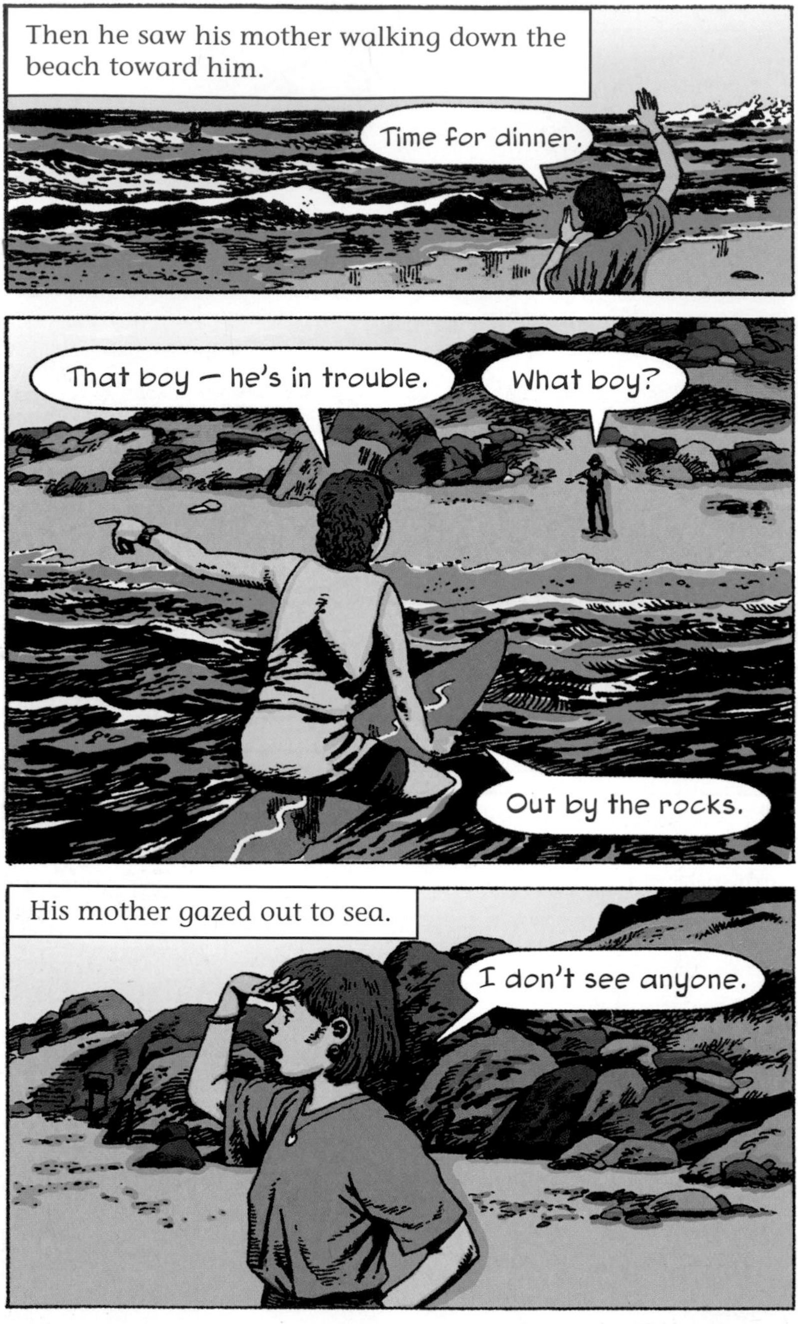
Then he saw his mother walking down the beach toward him.
Time for dinner.
That boy — he's in trouble.
What boy?
Out by the rocks.
His mother gazed out to sea.
I don't see anyone.

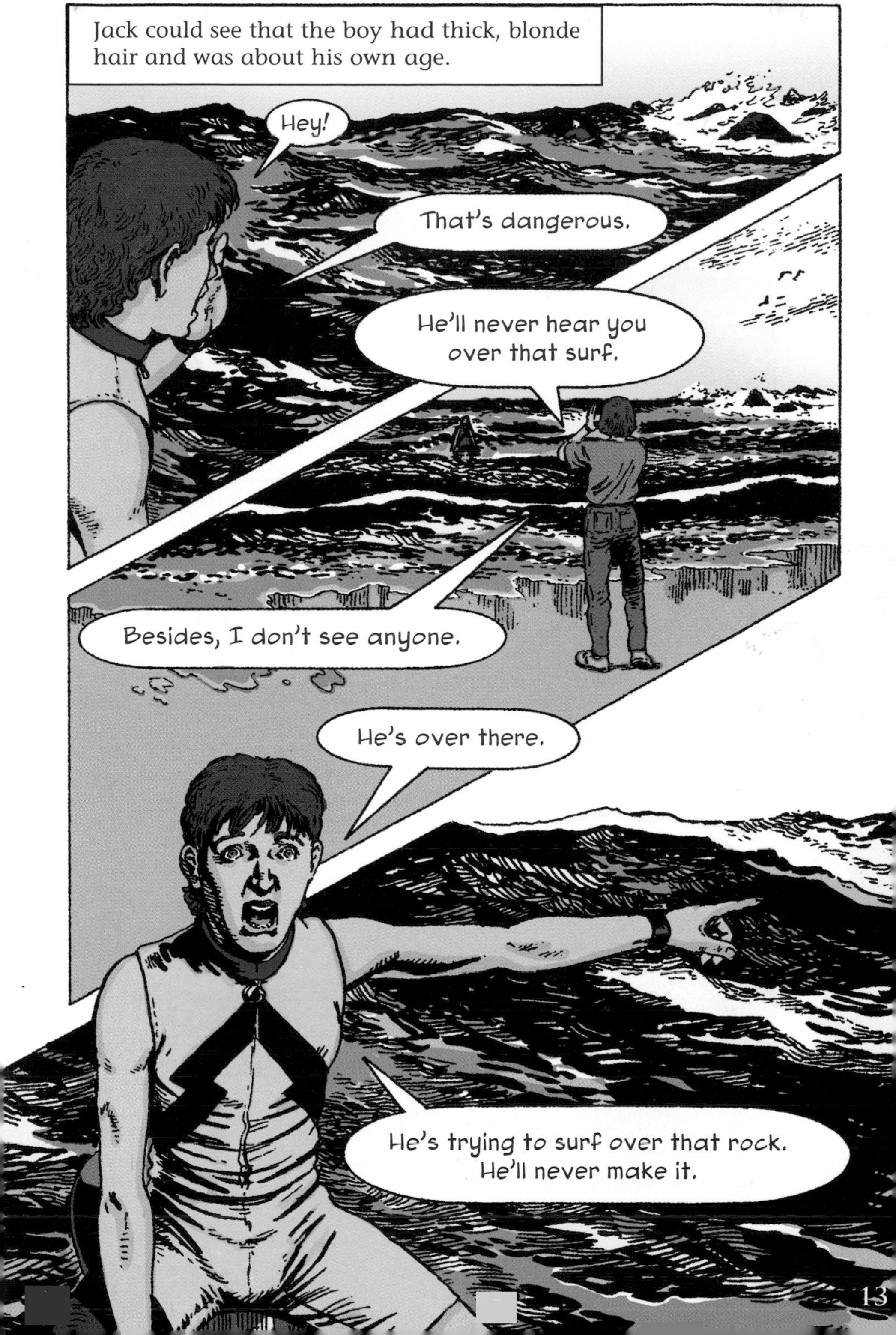
Jack could see that the boy had thick, blonde hair and was about his own age.
Hey!
That's dangerous.
He'll never hear you over that surf.
Besides, I don't see anyone.
He's over there.
He's trying to surf over that rock. He'll never make it.

The rock was partly submerged and clouded with spray, but Jack could see that it was covered with sharp barnacles.

Then the boy disappeared.

Call for help.

Where are you going?

He needs help. I've got to get out there!

Then you'll be in trouble, too. Stay here, Jack. You must stay here!

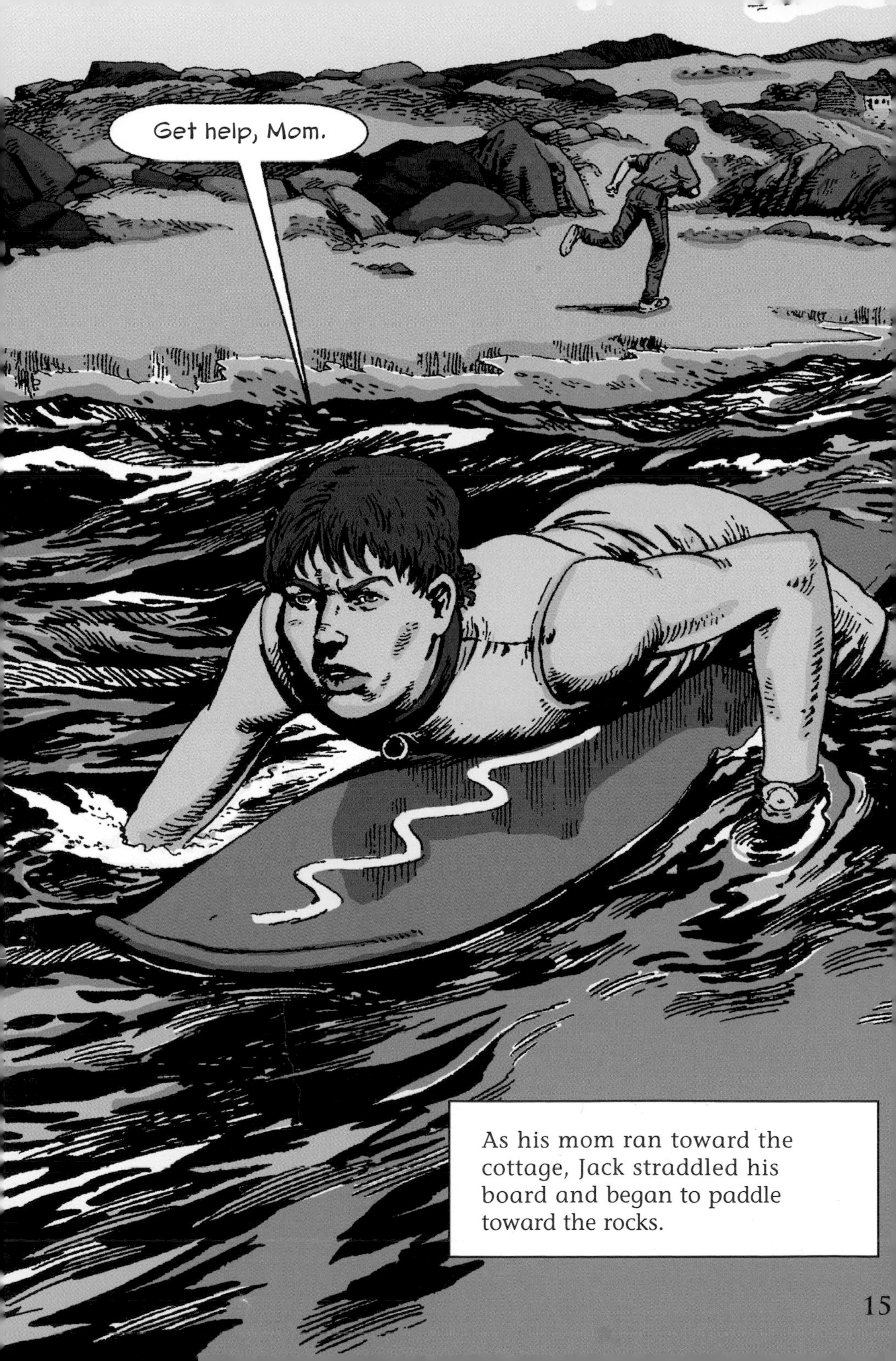
Get help, Mom.
As his mom ran toward the cottage, Jack straddled his board and began to paddle toward the rocks.

CHAPTER TWO

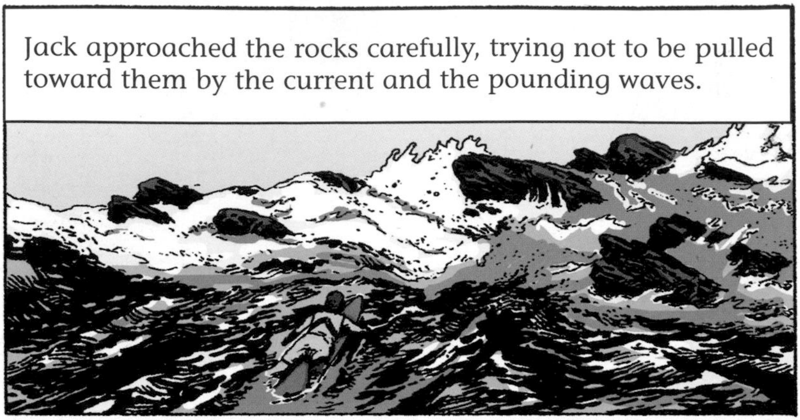
Jack approached the rocks carefully, trying not to be pulled toward them by the current and the pounding waves.

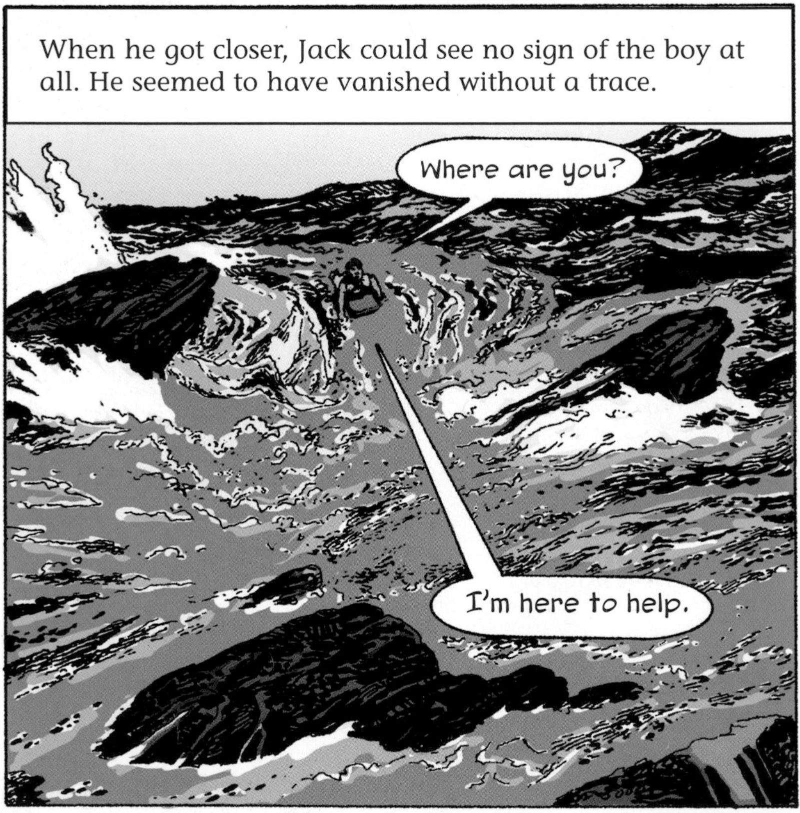
When he got closer, Jack could see no sign of the boy at all. He seemed to have vanished without a trace.
Where are you?
I'm here to help.

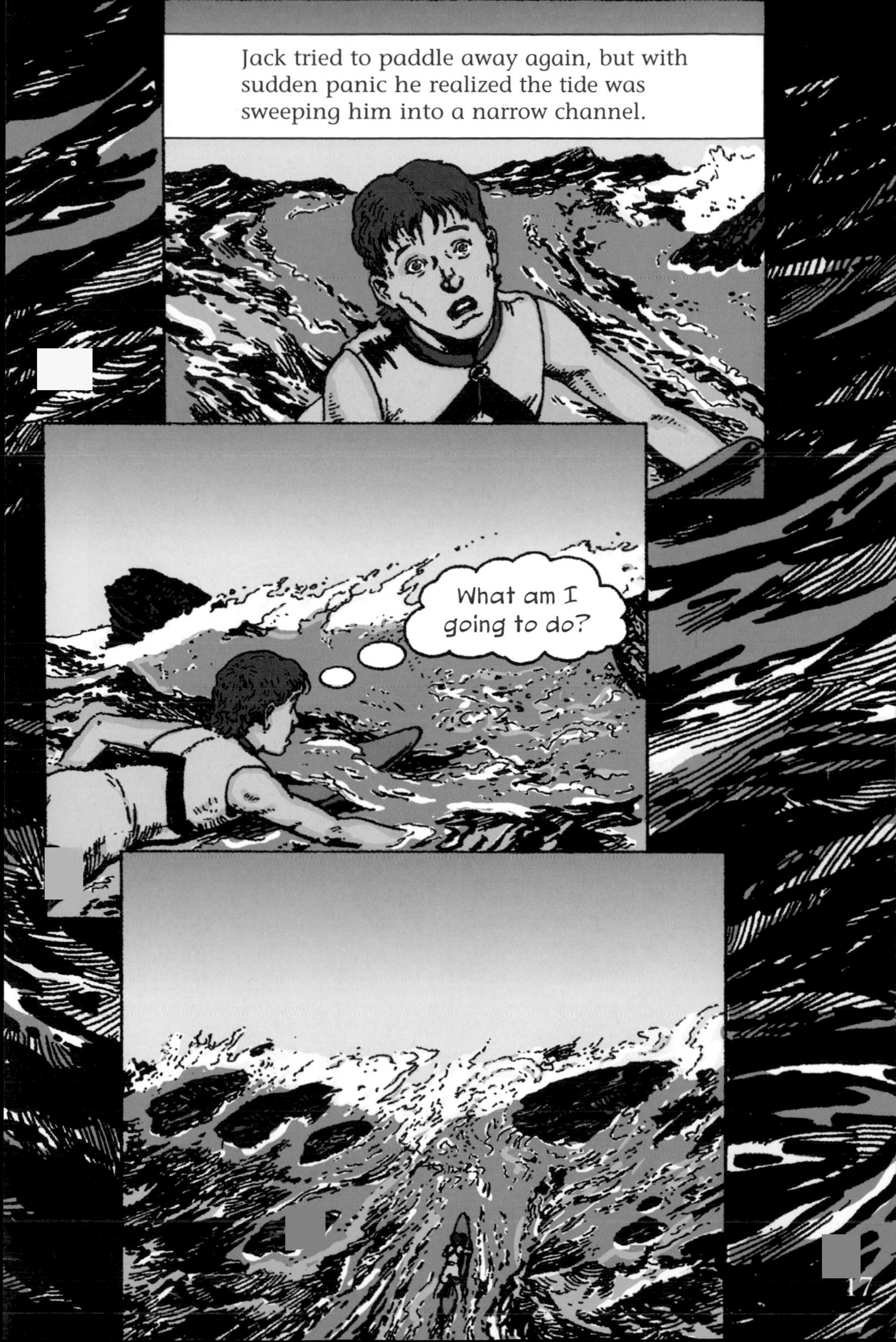
Jack tried to paddle away again, but with sudden panic he realized the tide was sweeping him into a narrow channel.
What am I going to do?

Suddenly, Jack saw a ledge above him. He grabbed at a mass of seaweed, kicked away his board, and pulled himself up.

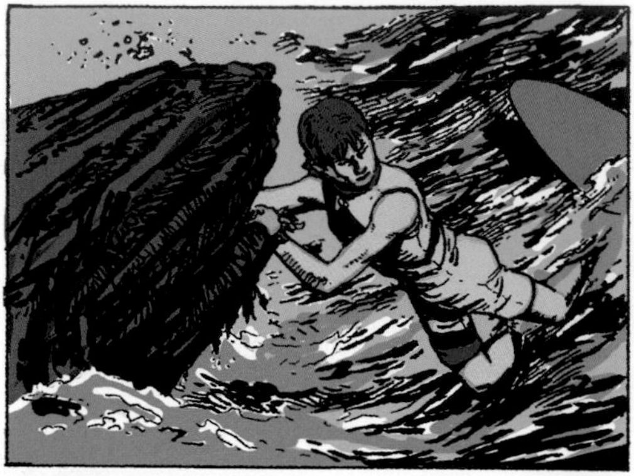

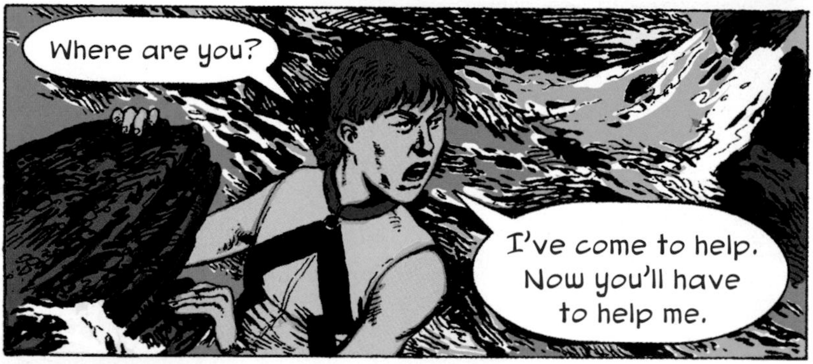
Where are you?
I've come to help. Now you'll have to help me.

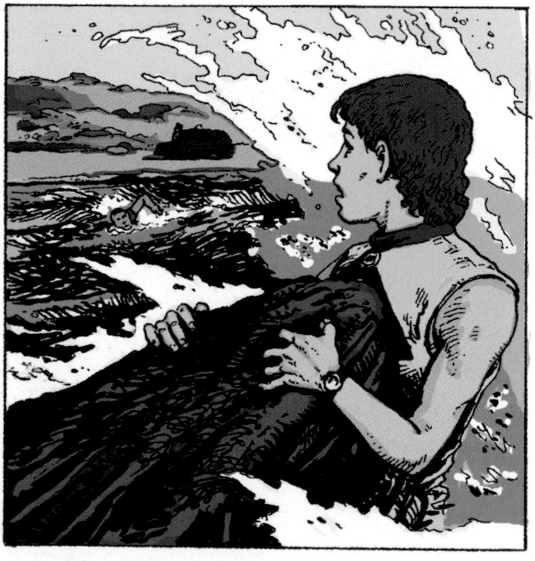

With relief, Jack saw someone swimming toward him. Through the spray he saw a jeep on the beach. It was a lifeguard, responding to his mother's emergency call.

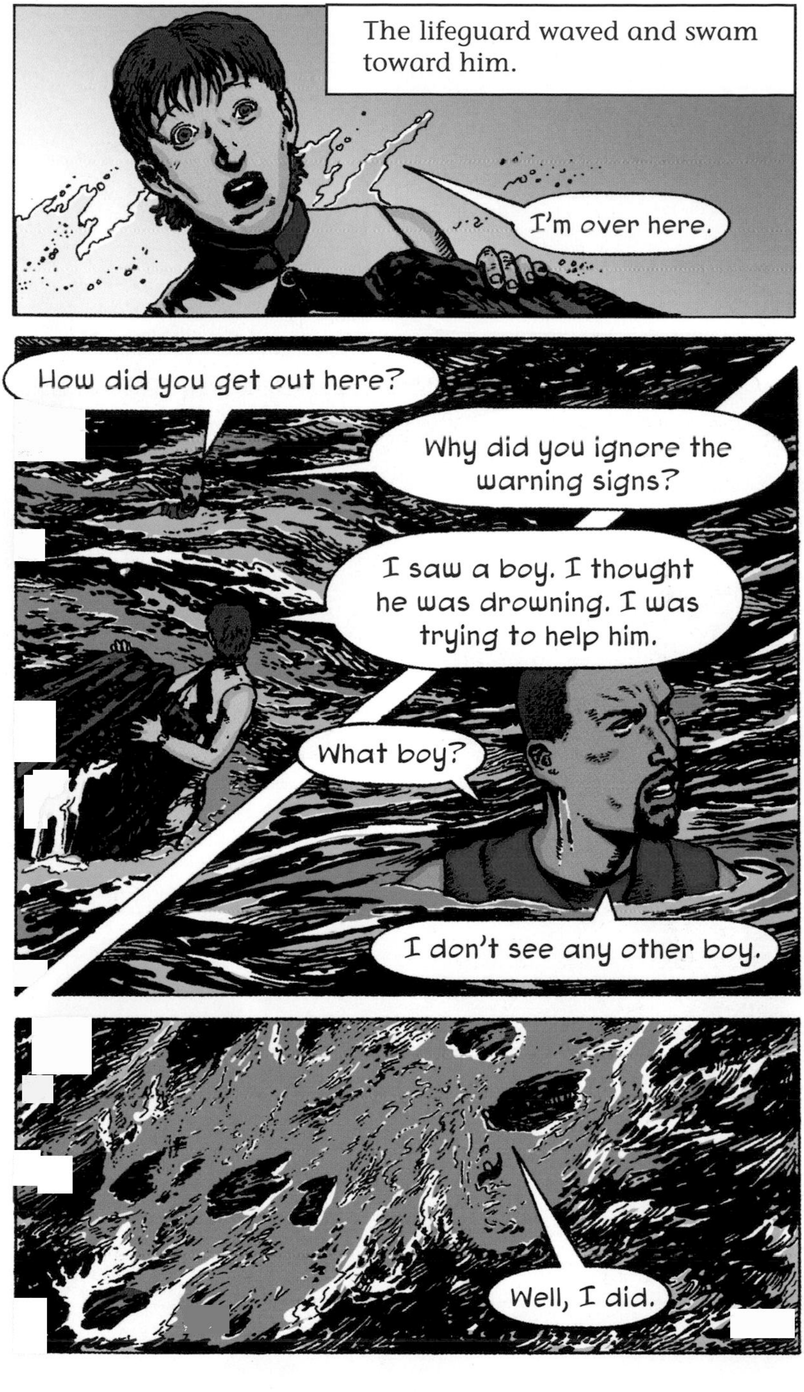
The lifeguard waved and swam toward him.
I'm over here.
How did you get out here?
Why did you ignore the warning signs?
I saw a boy. I thought he was drowning. I was trying to help him.
What boy?
I don't see any other boy.
Well, I did.

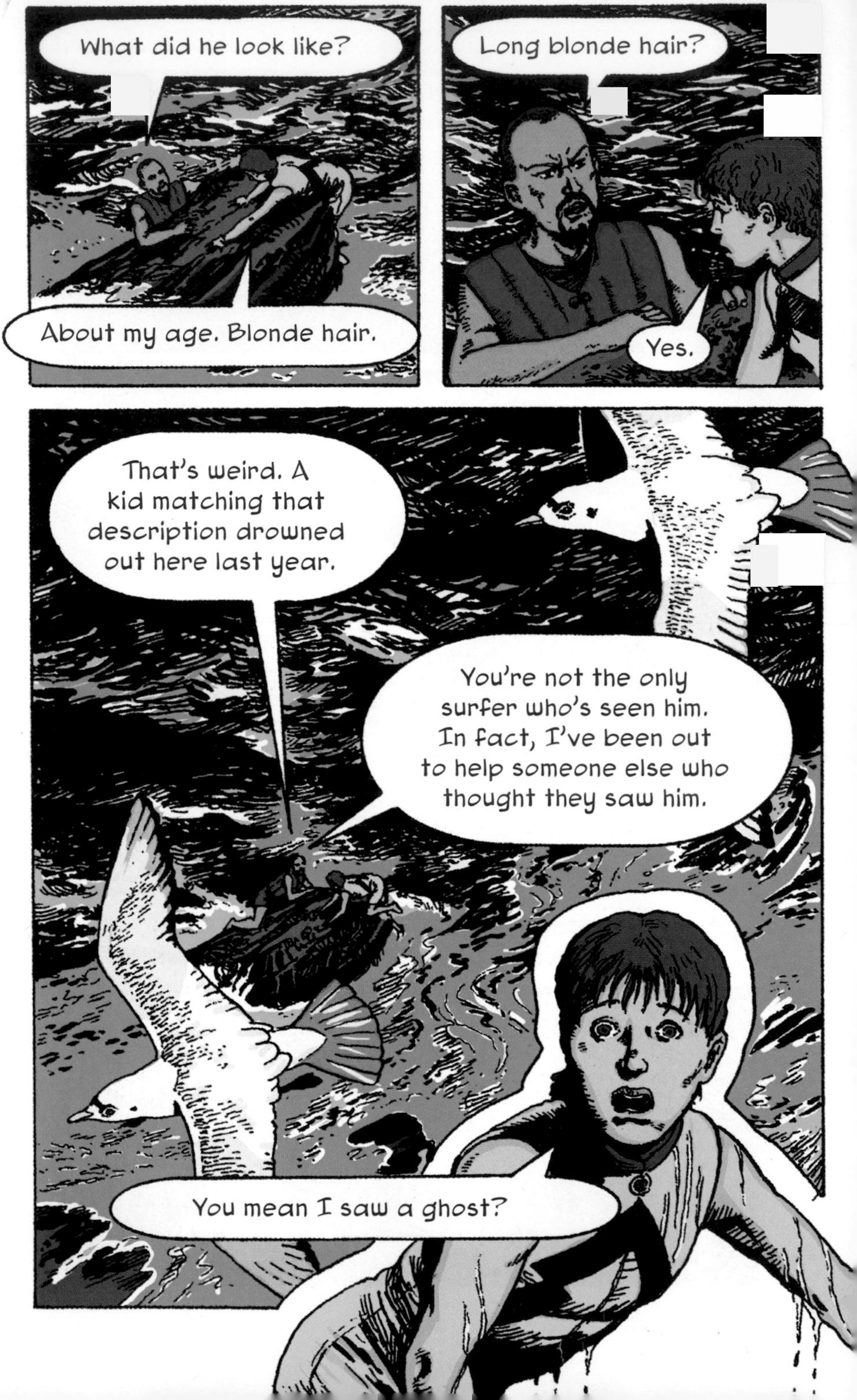
What did he look like?
About my age. Blonde hair.
Long blonde hair?
Yes.
That's weird. A kid matching that description drowned out here last year.
You're not the only surfer who's seen him. In fact, I've been out to help someone else who thought they saw him.
You mean I saw a ghost?

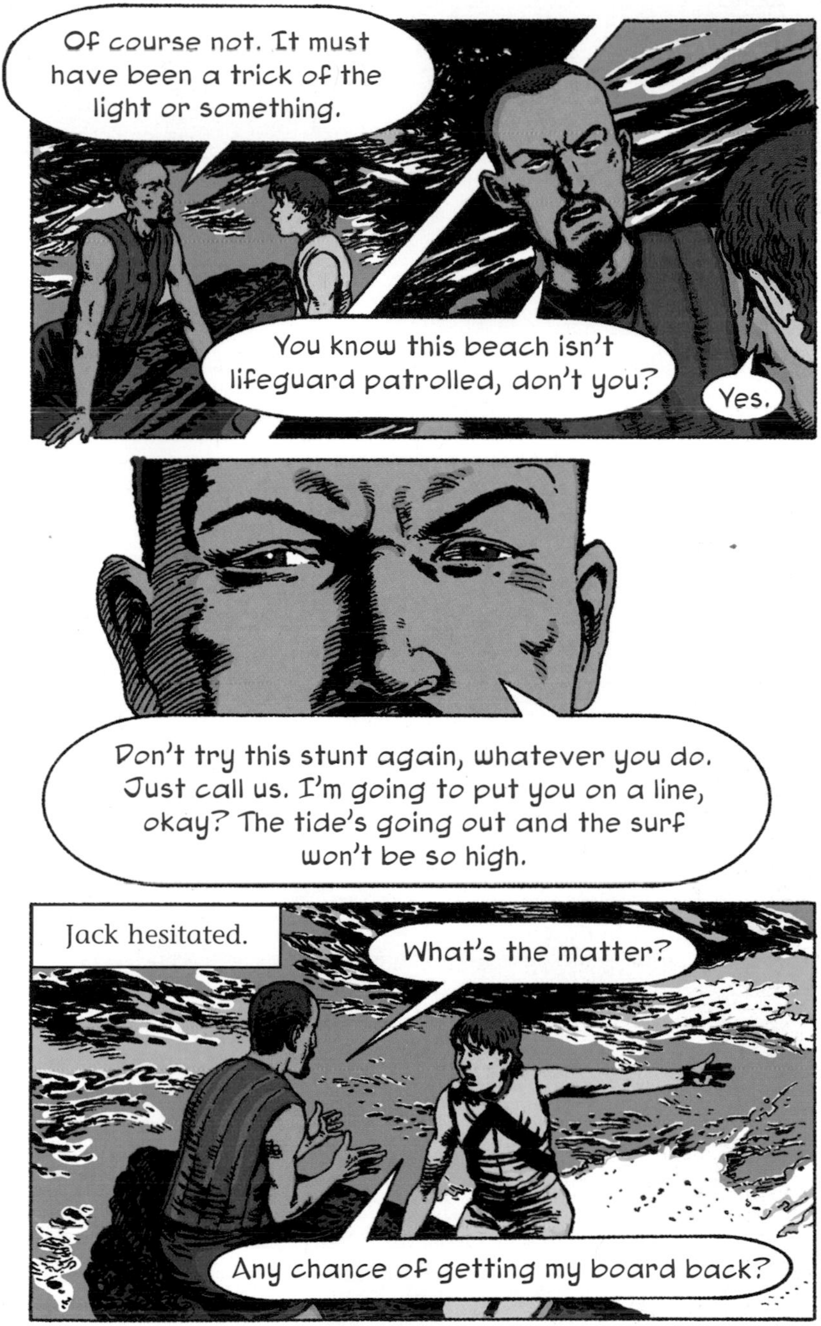
Of course not. It must have been a trick of the light or something.
You know this beach isn't lifeguard patrolled, don't you?
Yes.
Don't try this stunt again, whatever you do. Just call us. I'm going to put you on a line, okay? The tide's going out and the surf won't be so high.
Jack hesitated.
What's the matter?
Any chance of getting my board back?

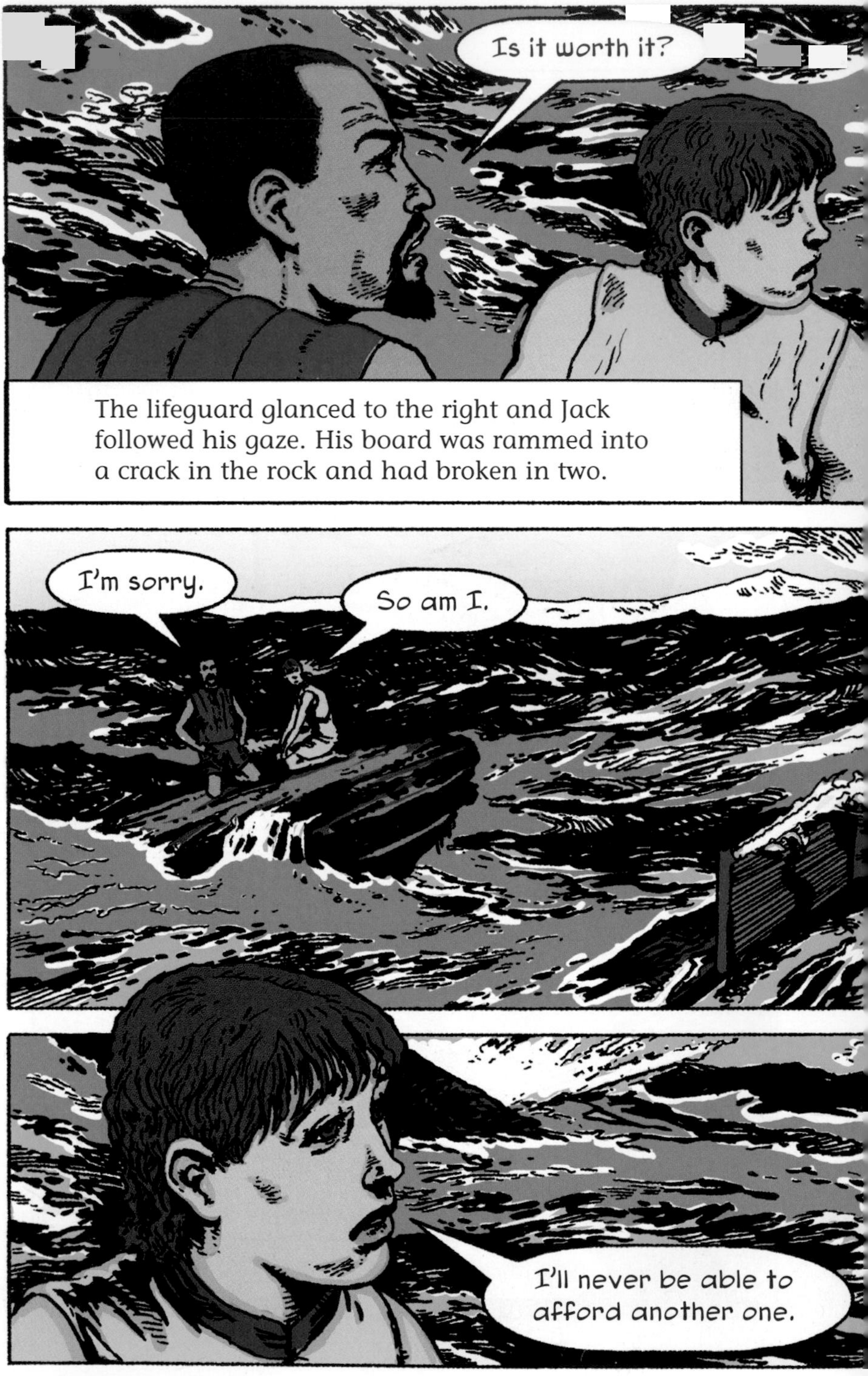
Is it worth it?
The lifeguard glanced to the right and Jack followed his gaze. His board was rammed into a crack in the rock and had broken in two.
I'm sorry.
So am I.
I'll never be able to afford another one.

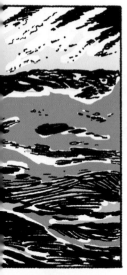

Once the lifeguard brought him back to the beach and gave him another safety lecture, he drove off. Mrs. Morton was angry and humiliated.

Of all the stupid, irresponsible things to do. You could have drowned out there.

I saw that boy.

No one else did.

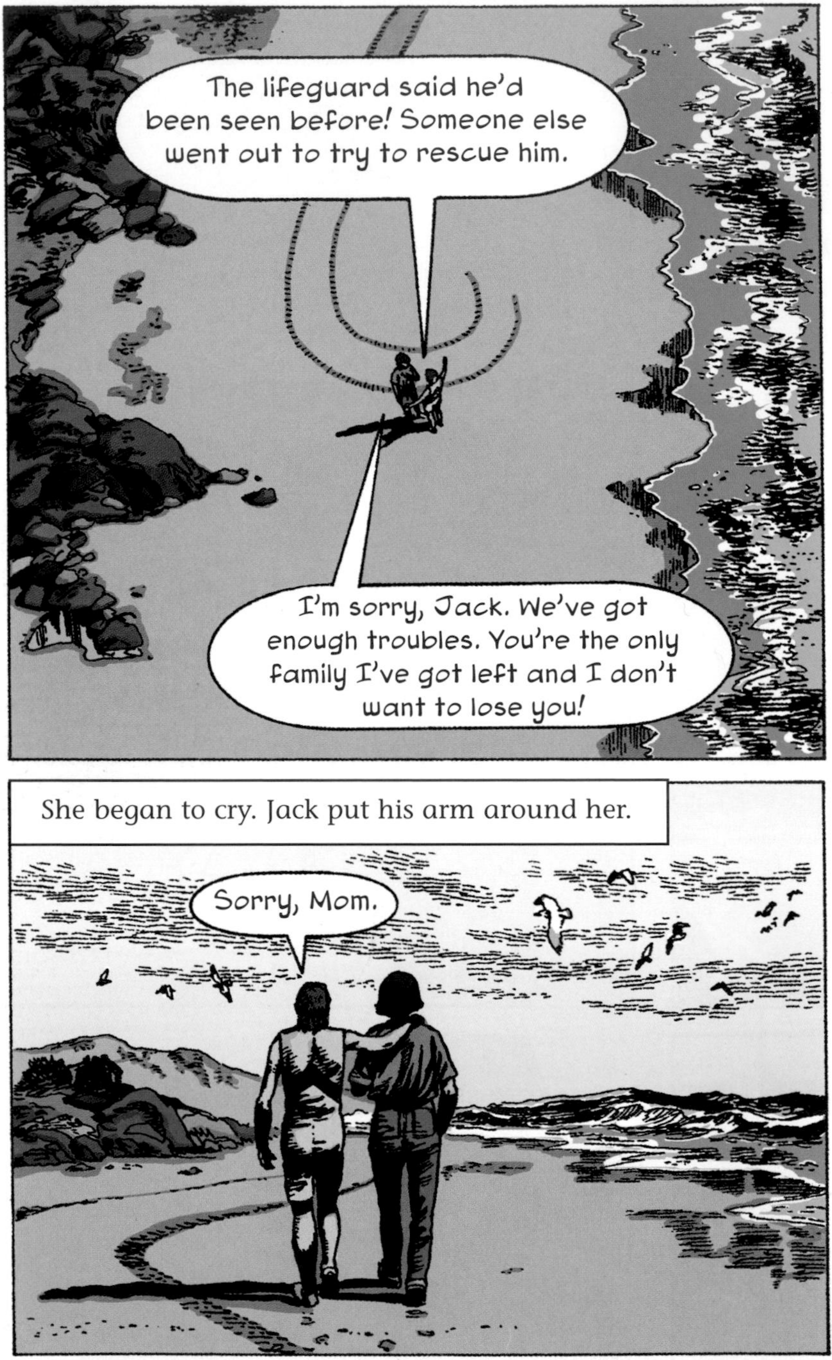
The lifeguard said he'd been seen before! Someone else went out to try to rescue him.
I'm sorry, Jack. We've got enough troubles. You're the only family I've got left and I don't want to lose you!
She began to cry. Jack put his arm around her.
Sorry, Mom.

CHAPTER THREE

The next evening . . .

If only I had a board. I'll never save up enough money to buy one this summer.

Jack felt sorry for himself. His dad had given him the board just before he left home. It was the only thing Jack had from him.

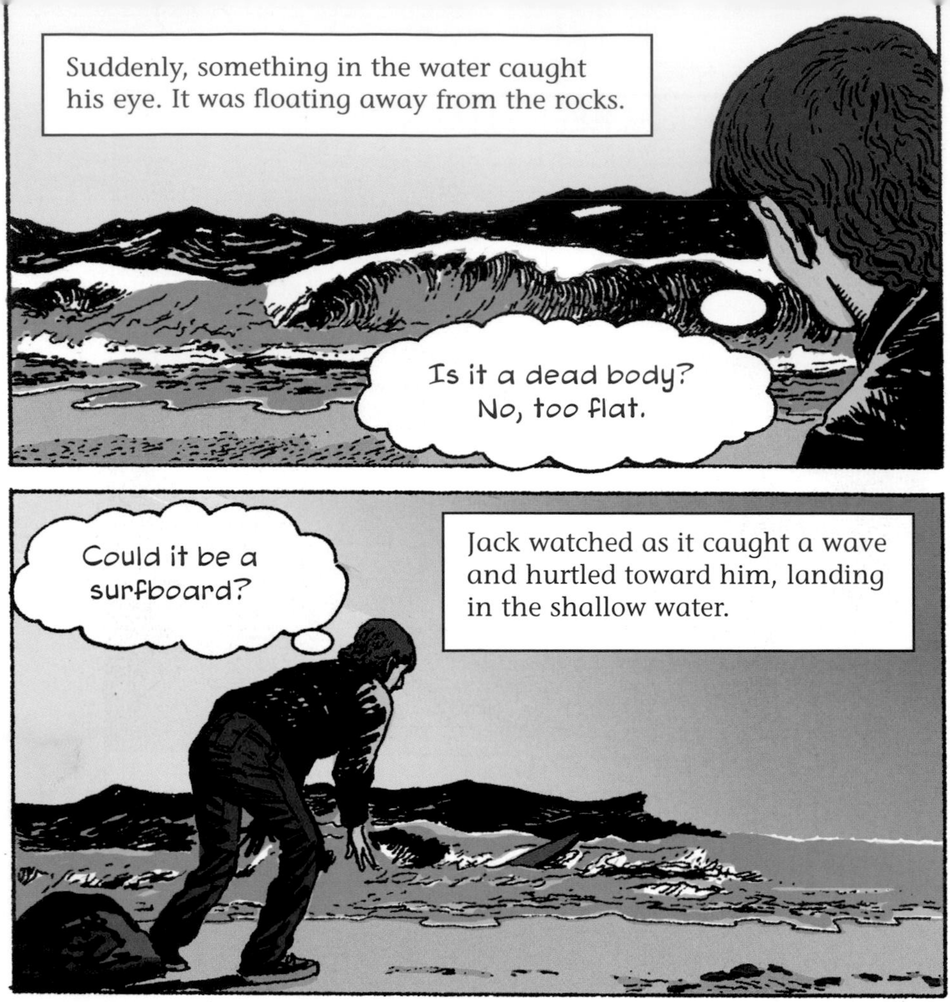
Suddenly, something in the water caught his eye. It was floating away from the rocks.
Is it a dead body? No, too flat.
Could it be a surfboard?
Jack watched as it caught a wave and hurtled toward him, landing in the shallow water.

Jack made a dash for it, pulling the surfboard up on the sand. The board was old and battered but beautifully waxed. Jack looked around. There was no one in sight, so he picked it up and headed for home.

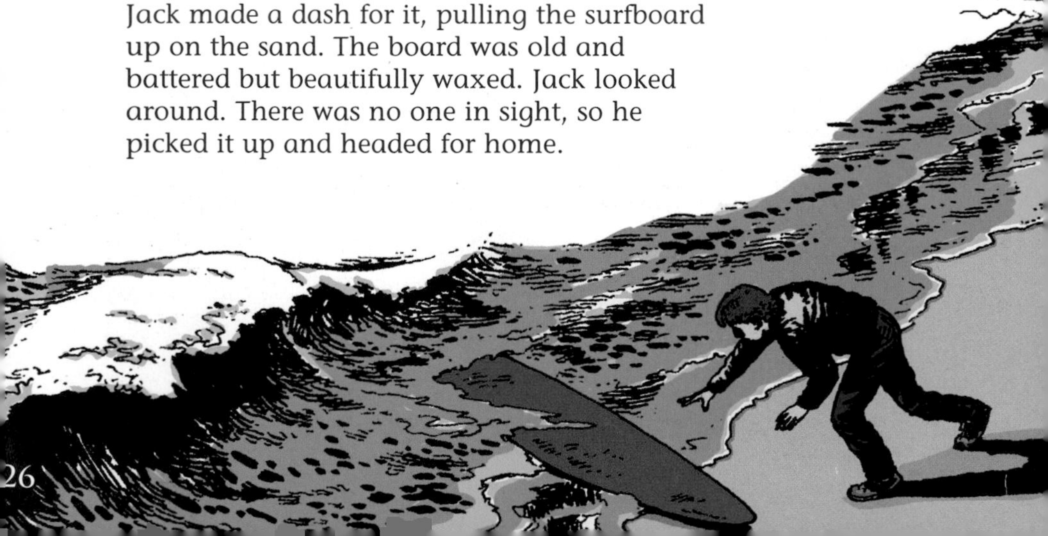

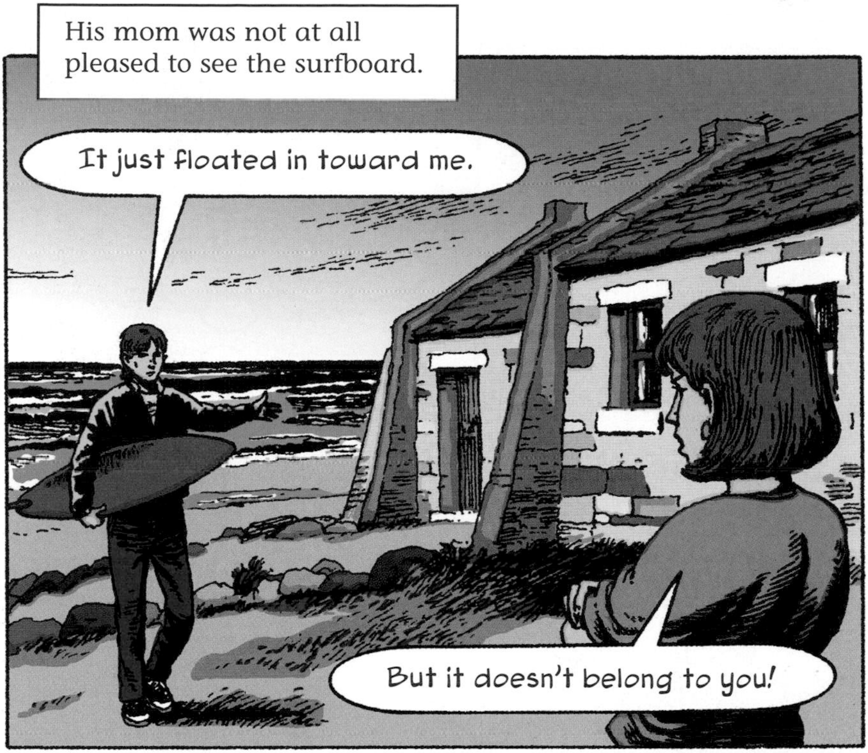
His mom was not at all pleased to see the surfboard.
It just floated in toward me.
But it doesn't belong to you!

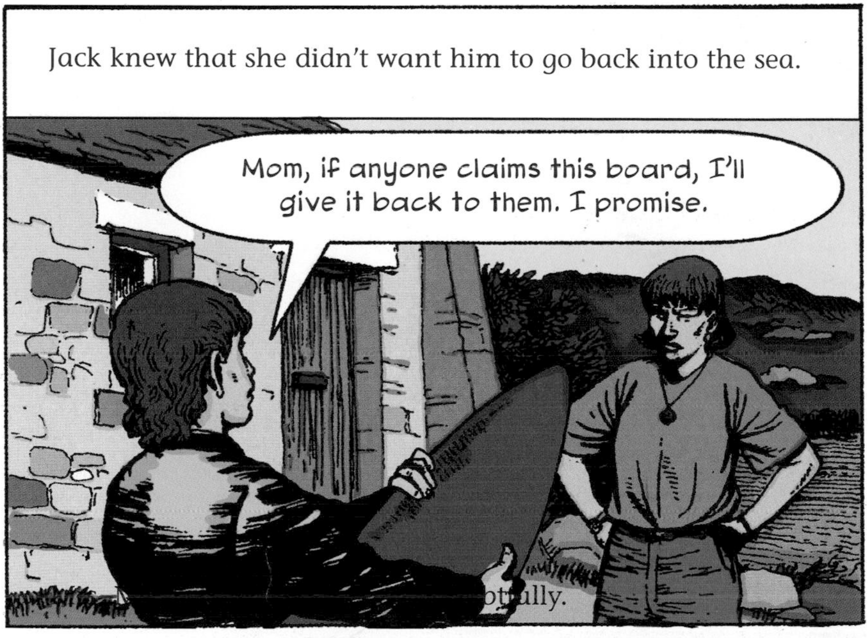
Jack knew that she didn't want him to go back into the sea.
Mom, if anyone claims this board, I'll give it back to them. I promise.

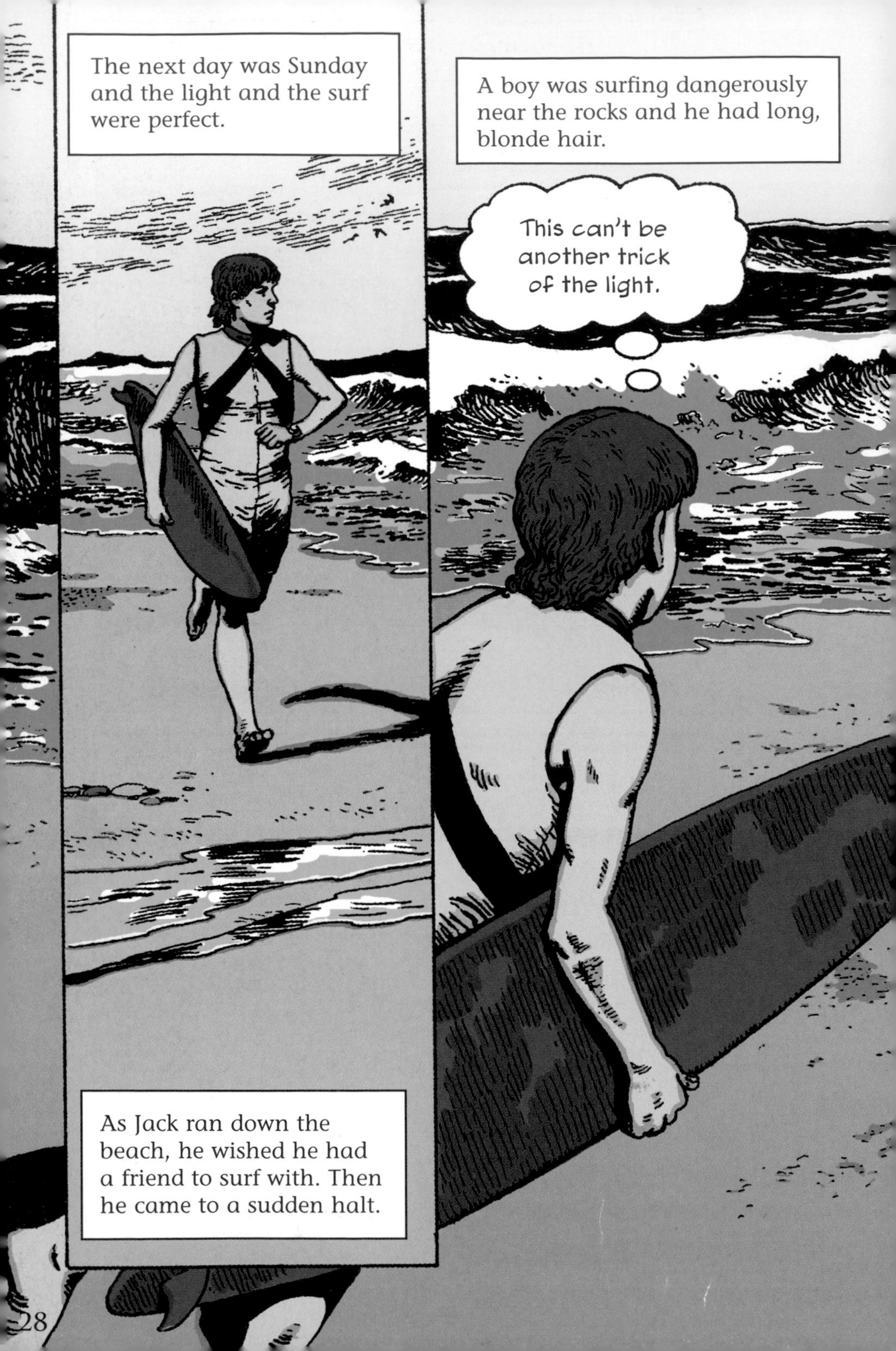
The next day was Sunday and the light and the surf were perfect.
As Jack ran down the beach, he wished he had a friend to surf with. Then he came to a sudden halt.
A boy was surfing dangerously near the rocks and he had long, blonde hair.
This can't be another trick of the light.

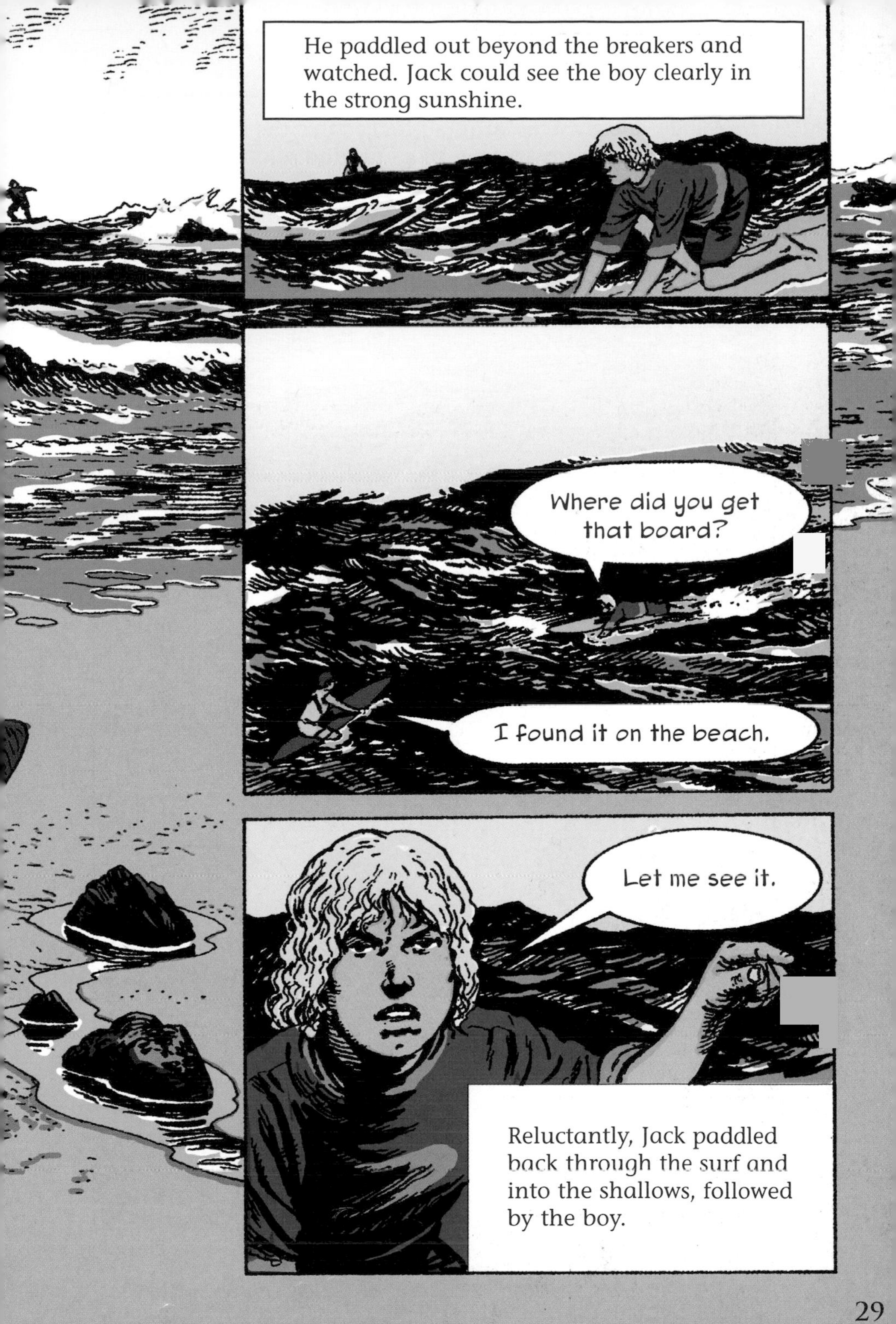
He paddled out beyond the breakers and watched. Jack could see the boy clearly in the strong sunshine.
Where did you get that board?
I found it on the beach.
Let me see it.
Reluctantly, Jack paddled back through the surf and into the shallows, followed by the boy.

Jack felt uneasy. This stranger looked like the boy he had seen yesterday. Was it all some kind of mistake?

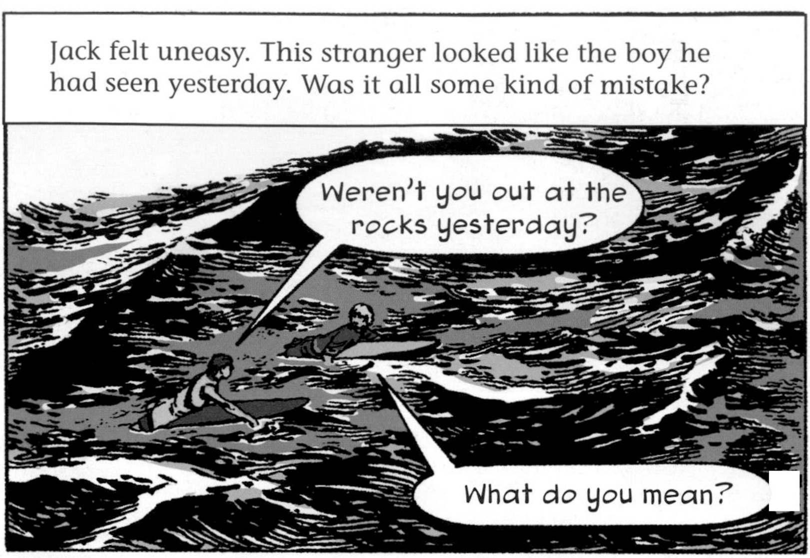
Weren't you out at the rocks yesterday?
What do you mean?

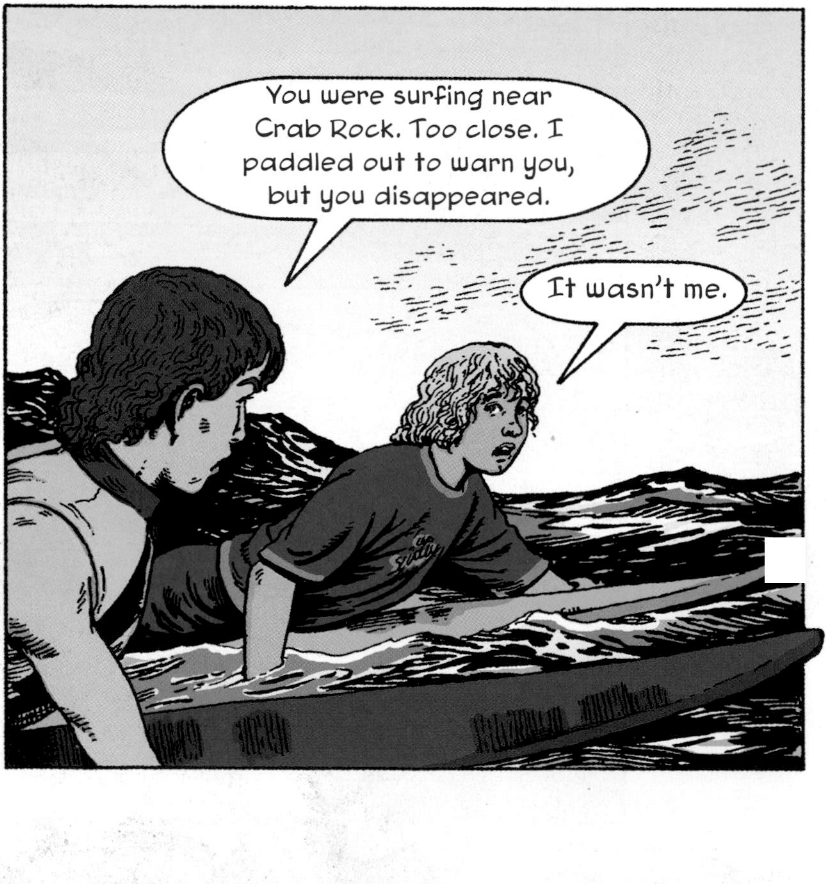
You were surfing near Crab Rock. Too close. I paddled out to warn you, but you disappeared.
It wasn't me.

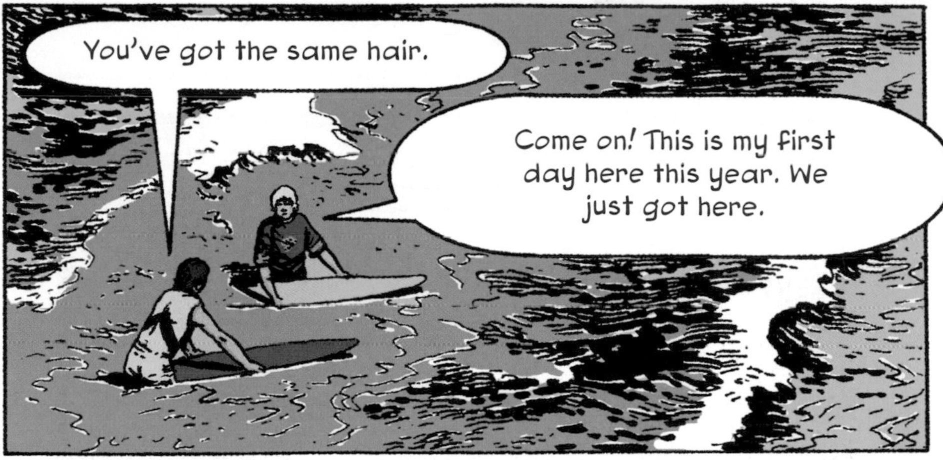
You've got the same hair.
Come on! This is my first day here this year. We just got here.

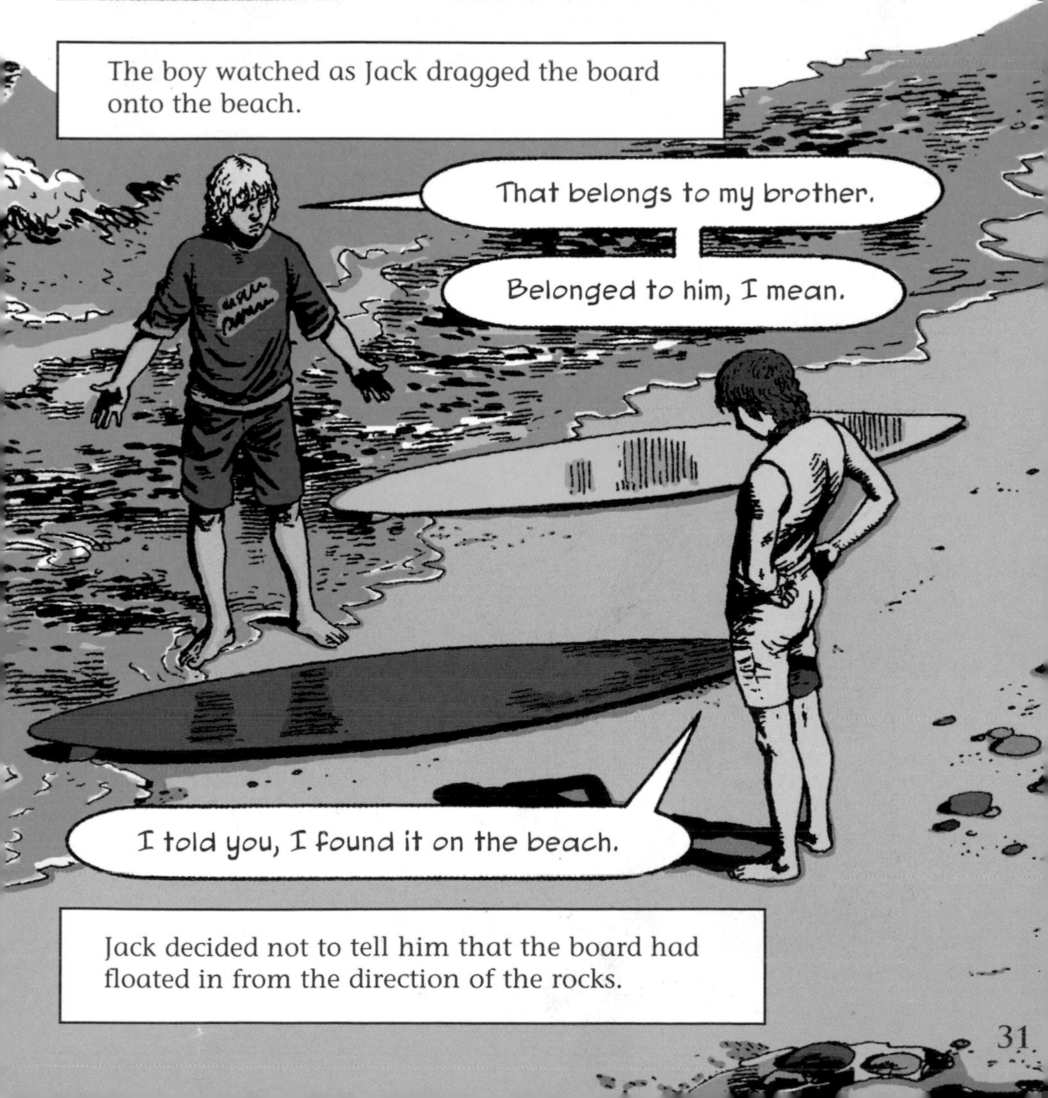
The boy watched as Jack dragged the board onto the beach.
That belongs to my brother.
Belonged to him, I mean.
I told you, I found it on the beach.
Jack decided not to tell him that the board had floated in from the direction of the rocks.

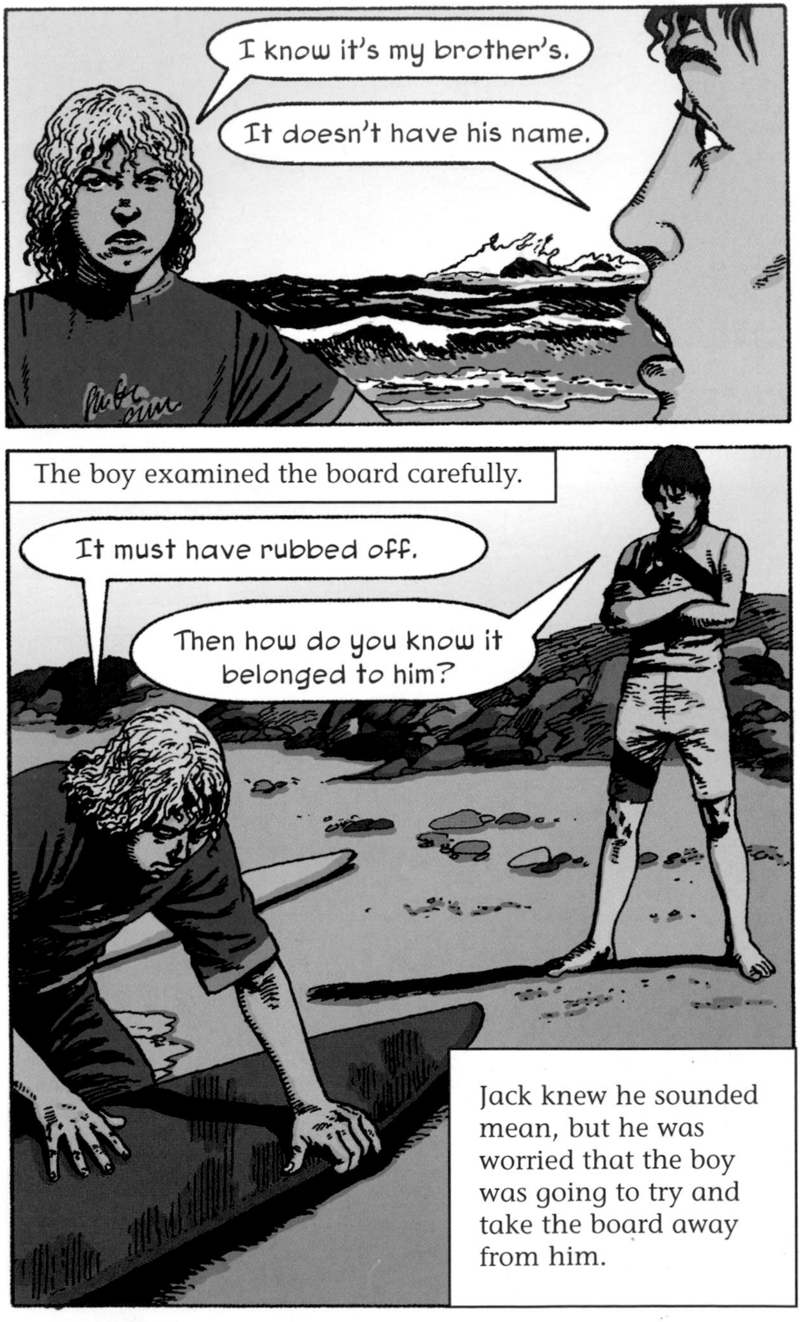
I know it's my brother's.
It doesn't have his name.
The boy examined the board carefully.
It must have rubbed off.
Then how do you know it belonged to him?
Jack knew he sounded mean, but he was worried that the boy was going to try and take the board away from him.

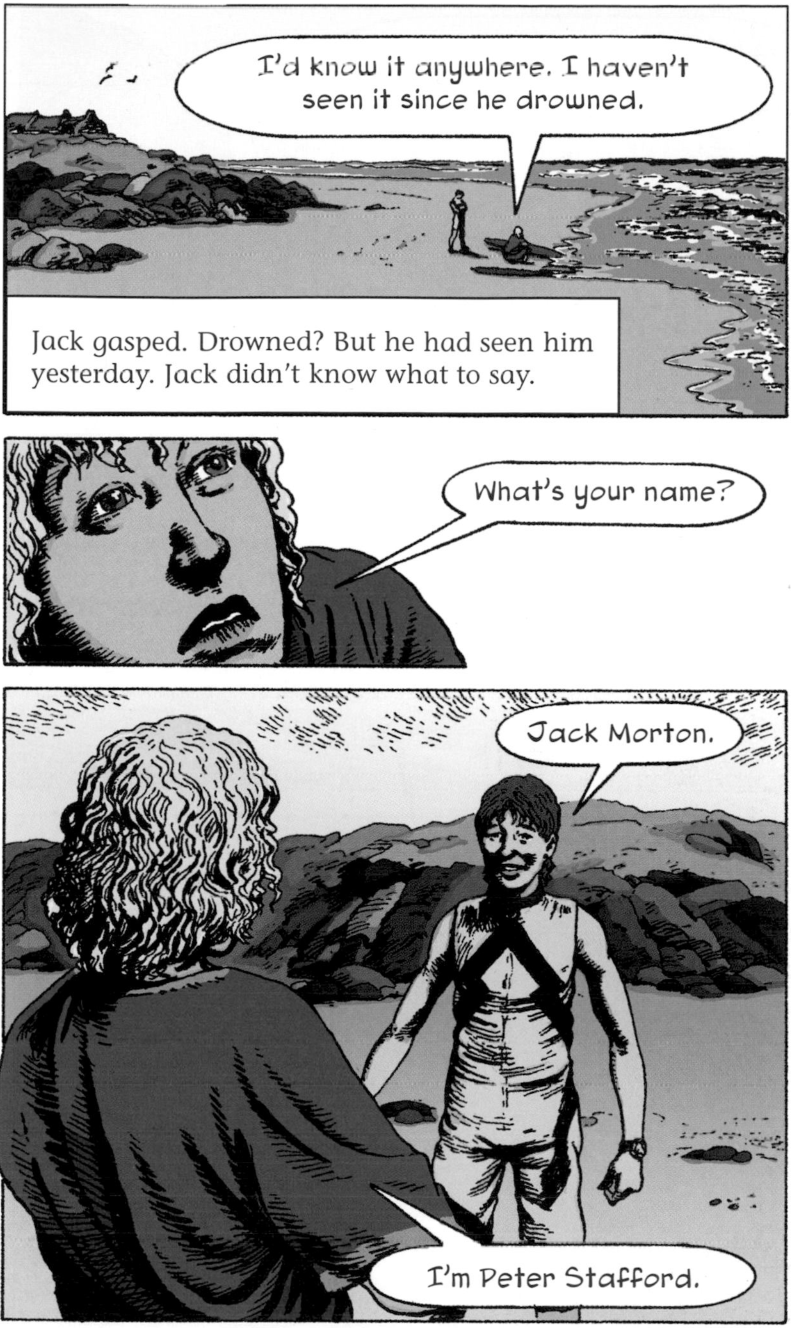
I'd know it anywhere. I haven't seen it since he drowned.
Jack gasped. Drowned? But he had seen him yesterday. Jack didn't know what to say.
What's your name?
Jack Morton.
I'm Peter Stafford.

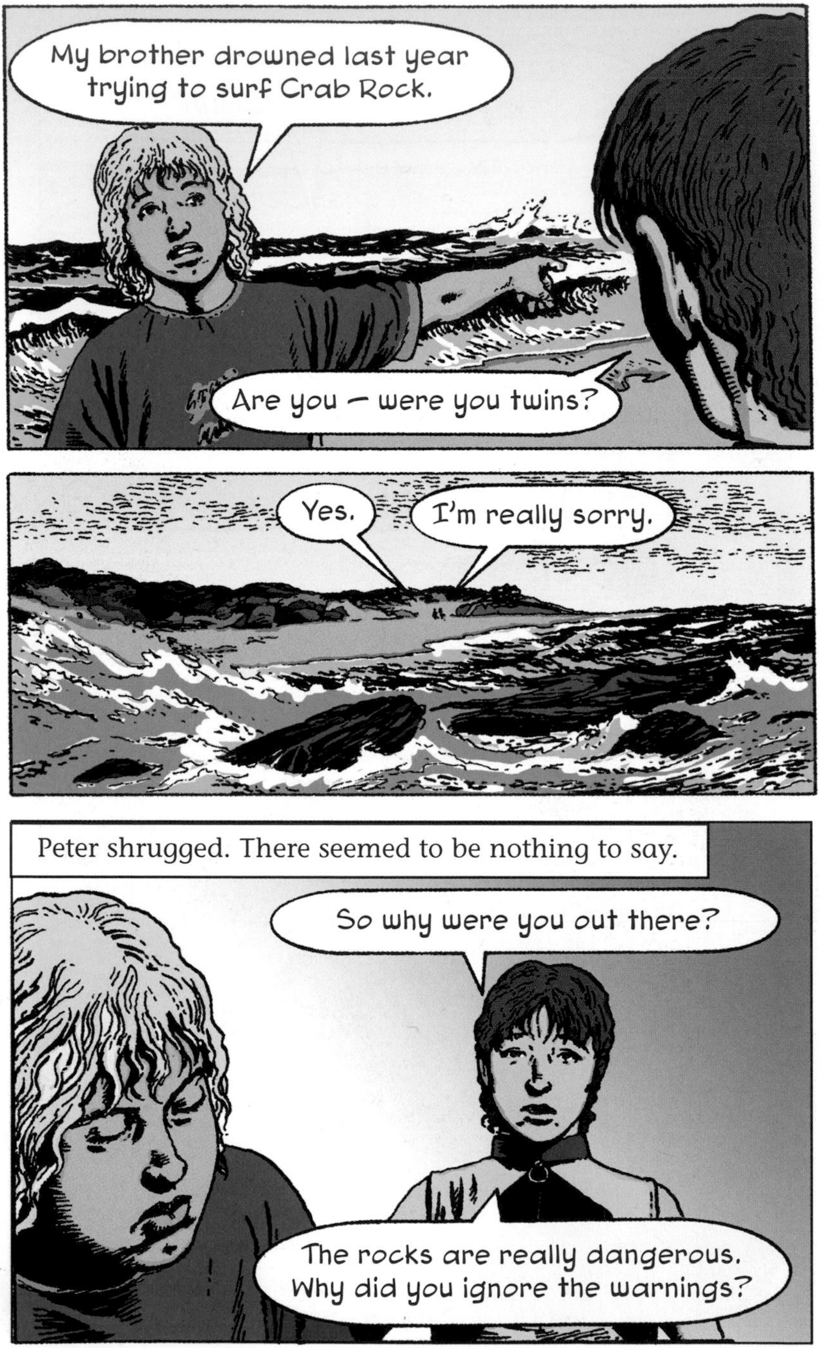
My brother drowned last year trying to surf Crab Rock.
Are you — were you twins?
Yes.
I'm really sorry.
Peter shrugged. There seemed to be nothing to say.
So why were you out there?
The rocks are really dangerous. Why did you ignore the warnings?

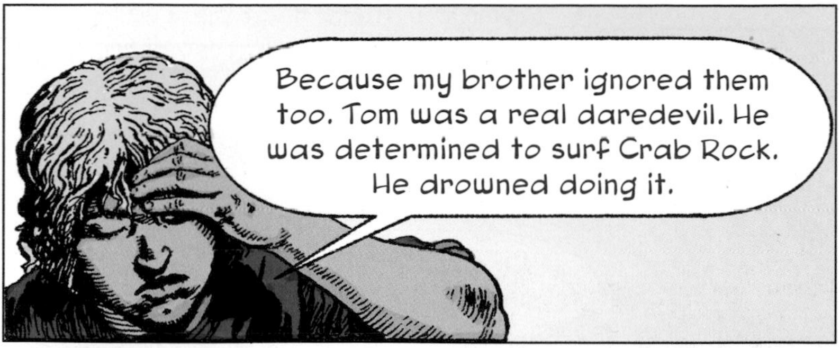
Because my brother ignored them too. Tom was a real daredevil. He was determined to surf Crab Rock. He drowned doing it.

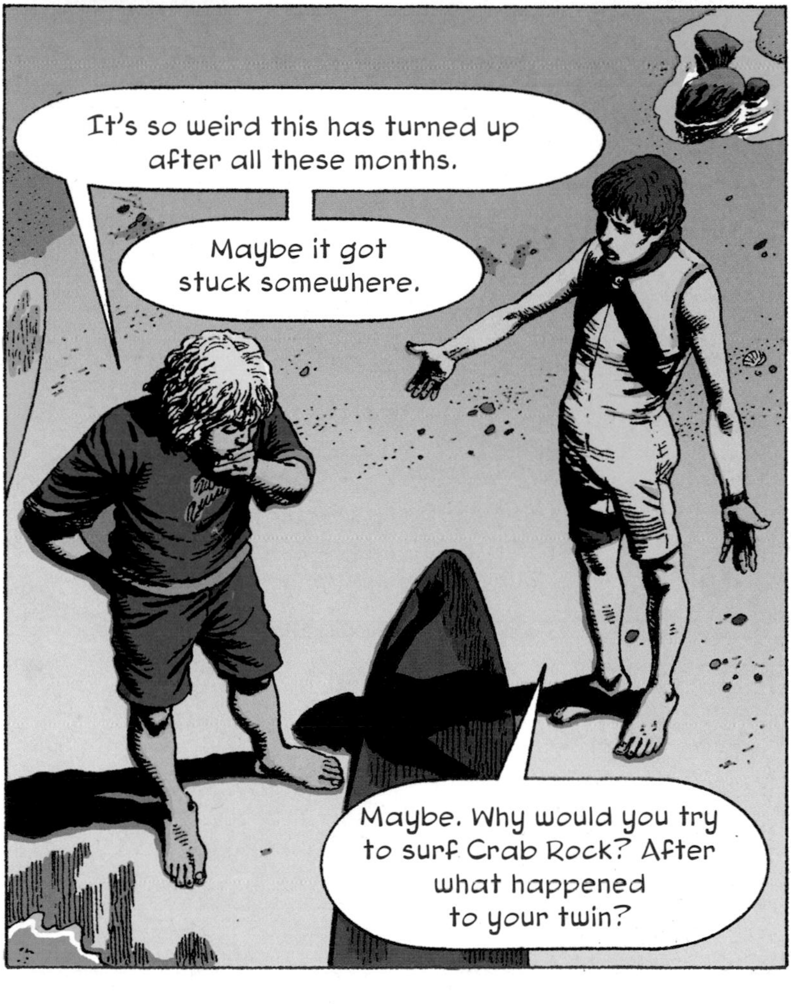
It's so weird this has turned up after all these months.
Maybe it got stuck somewhere.
Maybe. Why would you try to surf Crab Rock? After what happened to your twin?

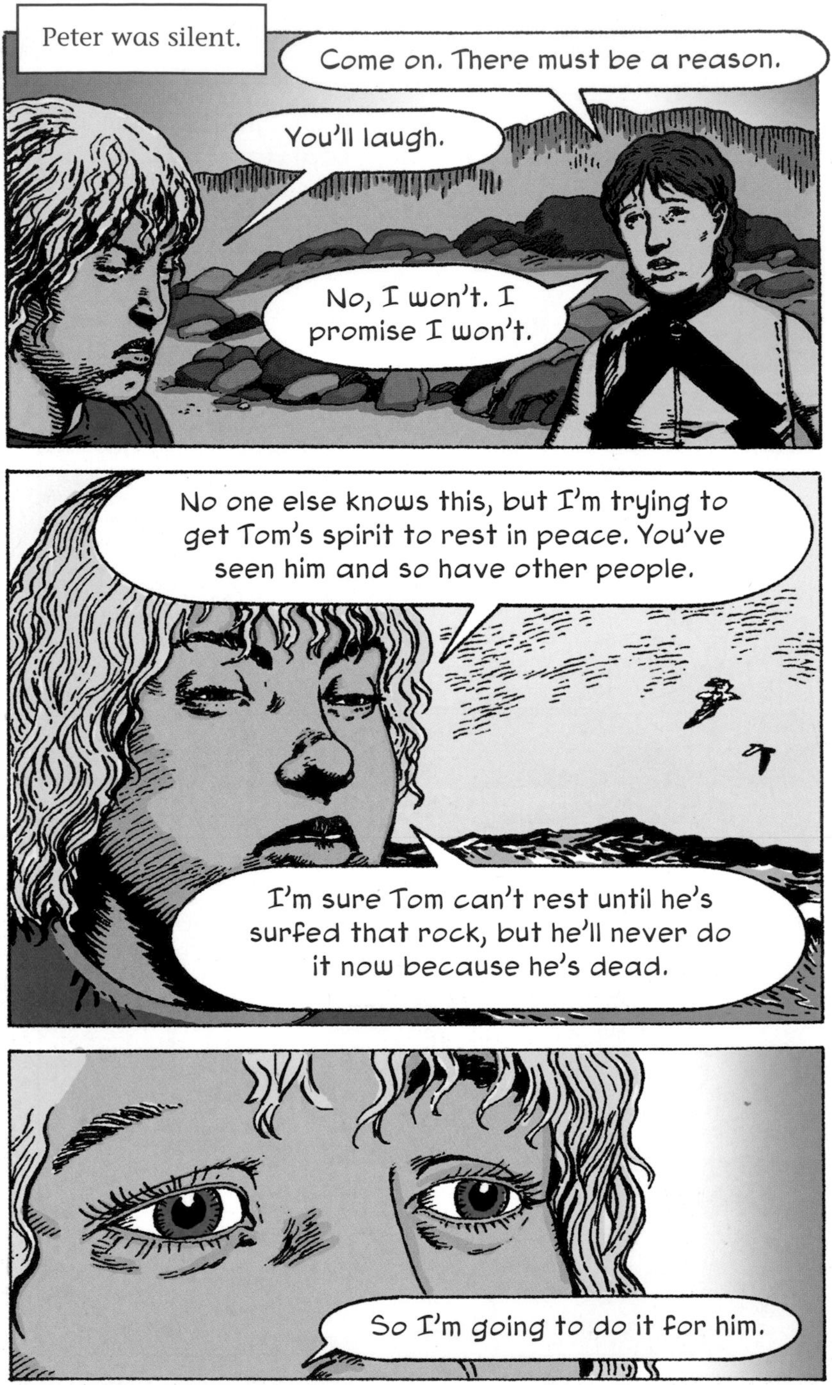
Peter was silent.
Come on. There must be a reason.
You'll laugh.
No, I won't. I promise I won't.
No one else knows this, but I'm trying to get Tom's spirit to rest in peace. You've seen him and so have other people.
I'm sure Tom can't rest until he's surfed that rock, but he'll never do it now because he's dead.
So I'm going to do it for him.

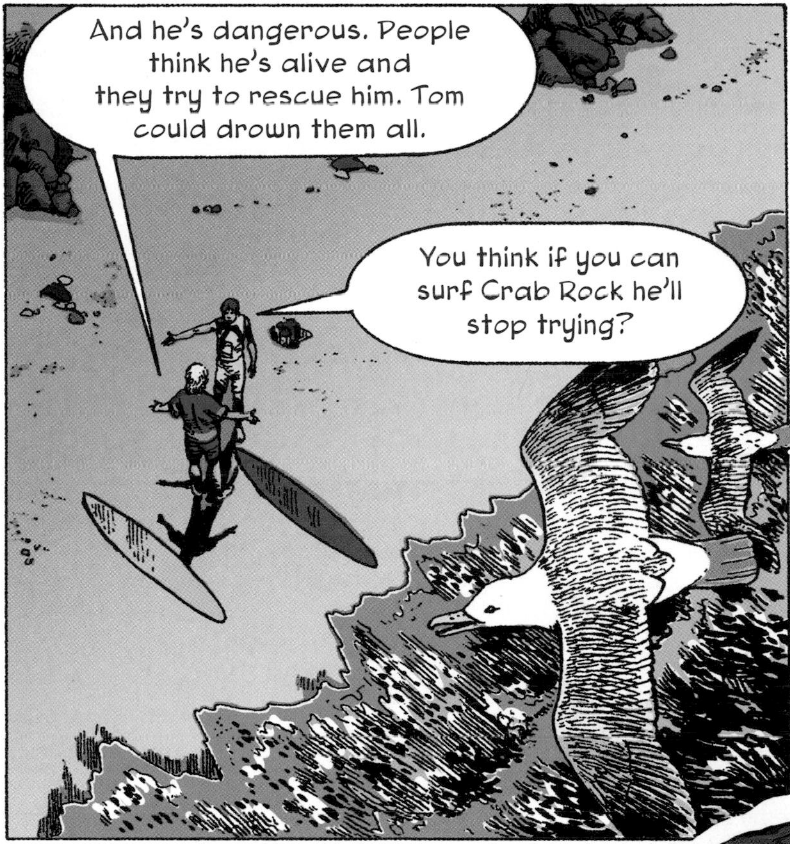
And he's dangerous. People think he's alive and they try to rescue him. Tom could drown them all.
You think if you can surf Crab Rock he'll stop trying?

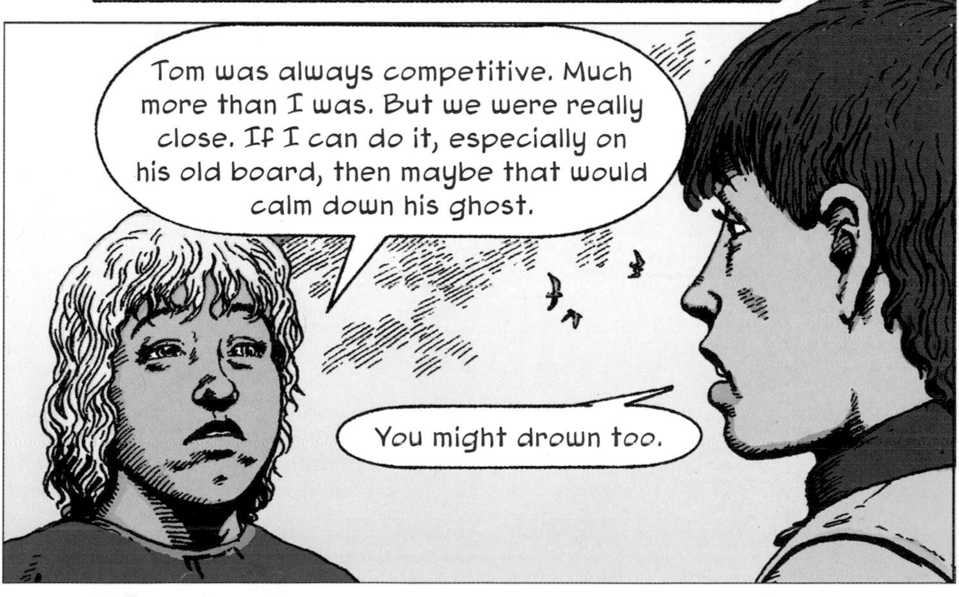
Tom was always competitive. Much more than I was. But we were really close. If I can do it, especially on his old board, then maybe that would calm down his ghost.
You might drown too.

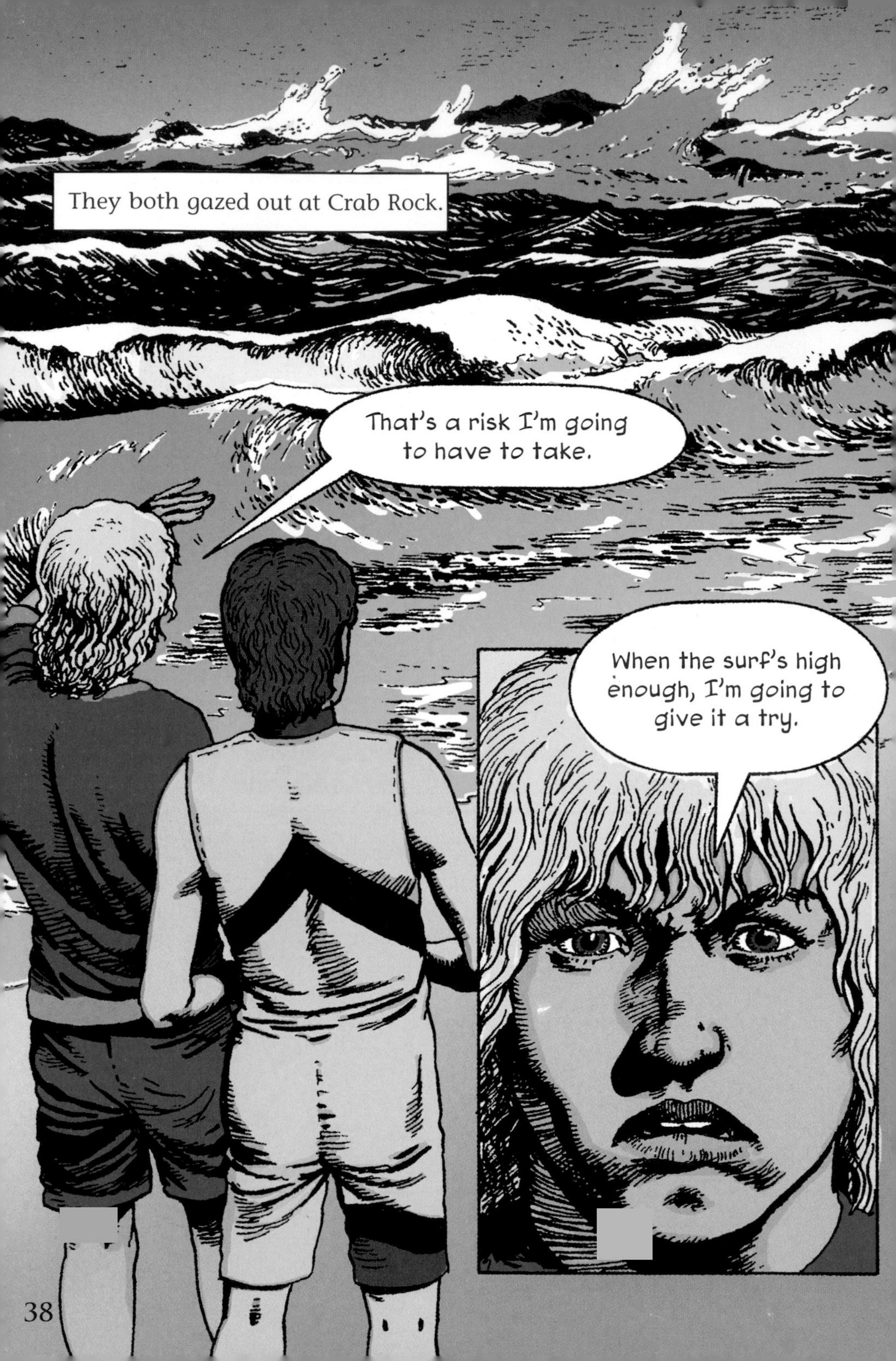
They both gazed out at Crab Rock.
That's a risk I'm going to have to take.
When the surf's high enough, I'm going to give it a try.

CHAPTER FOUR

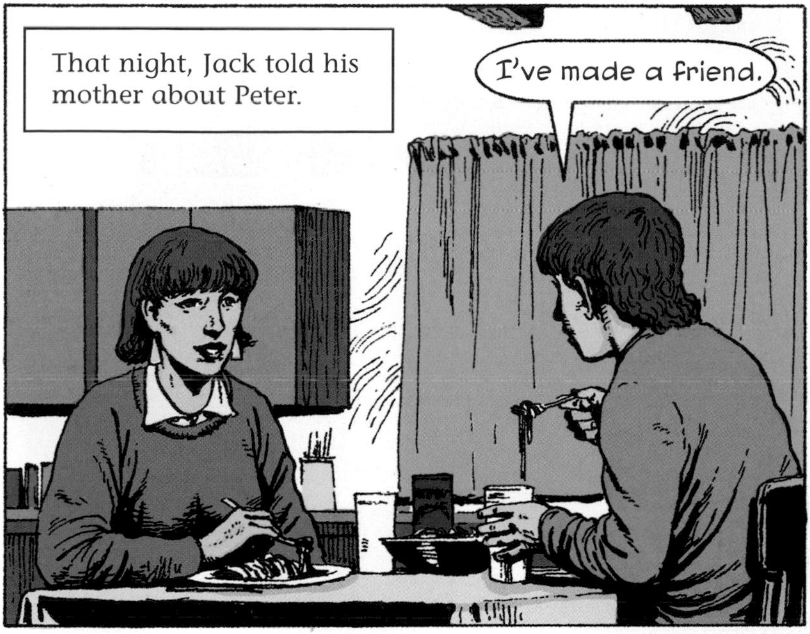
That night, Jack told his mother about Peter.
I've made a friend.

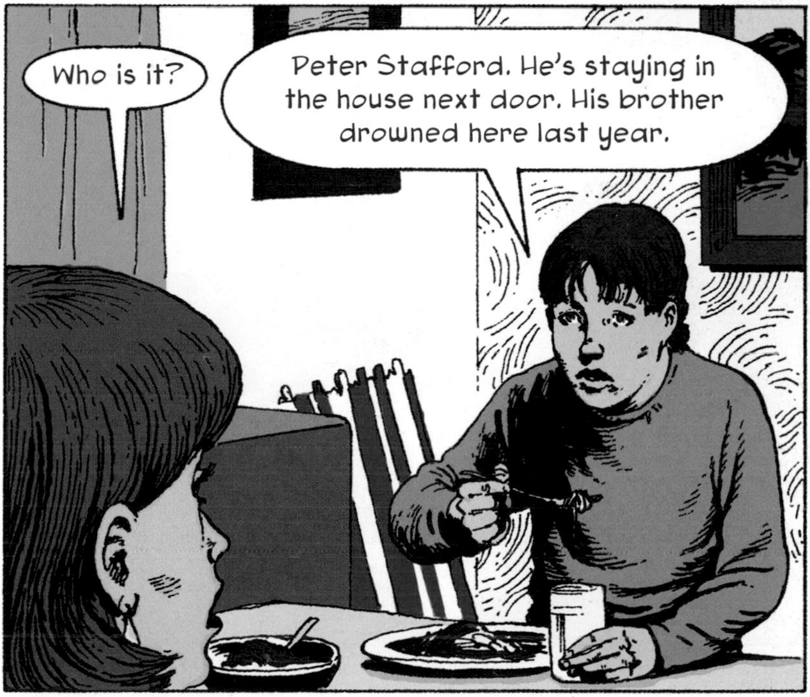
Who is it?
Peter Stafford. He's staying in the house next door. His brother drowned here last year.

Mrs. Morton gave Jack a strange look.

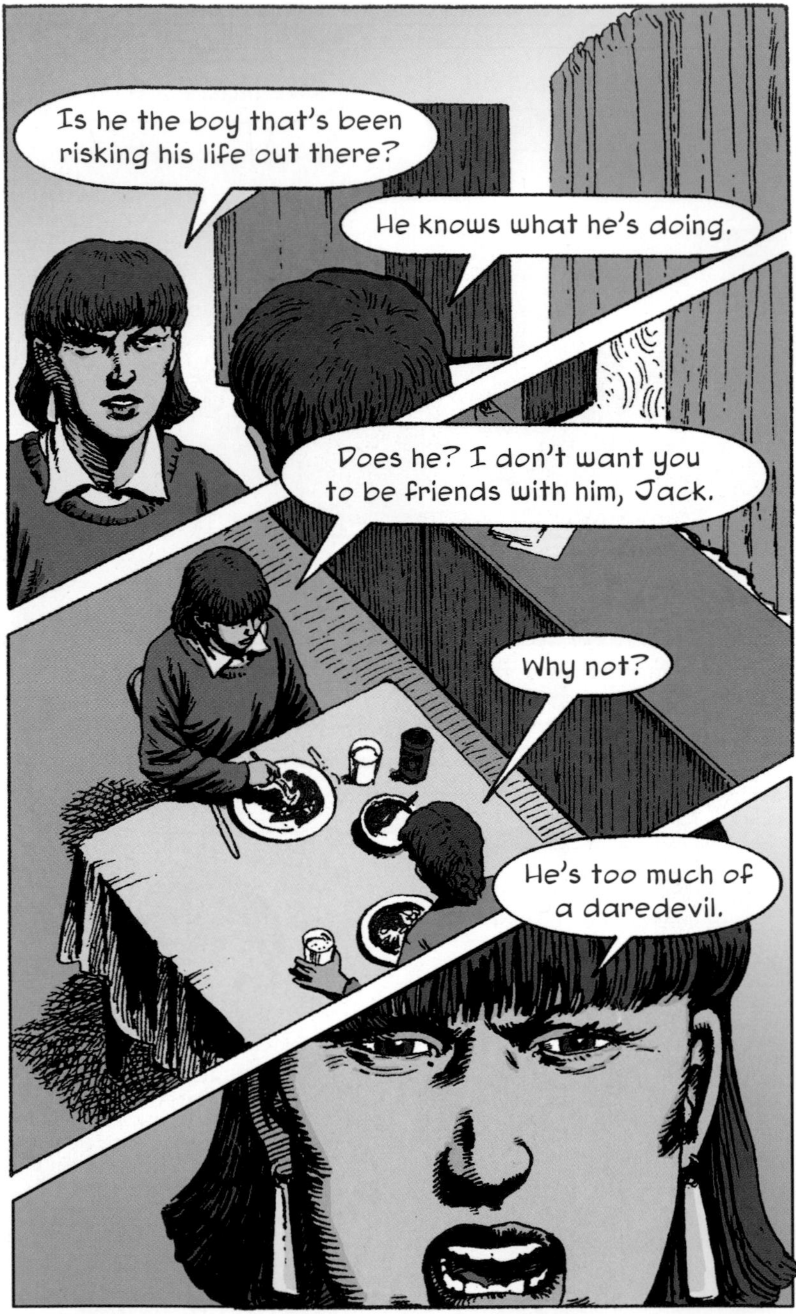

Is he the boy that's been risking his life out there?
He knows what he's doing.
Does he? I don't want you to be friends with him, Jack.
Why not?
He's too much of a daredevil.

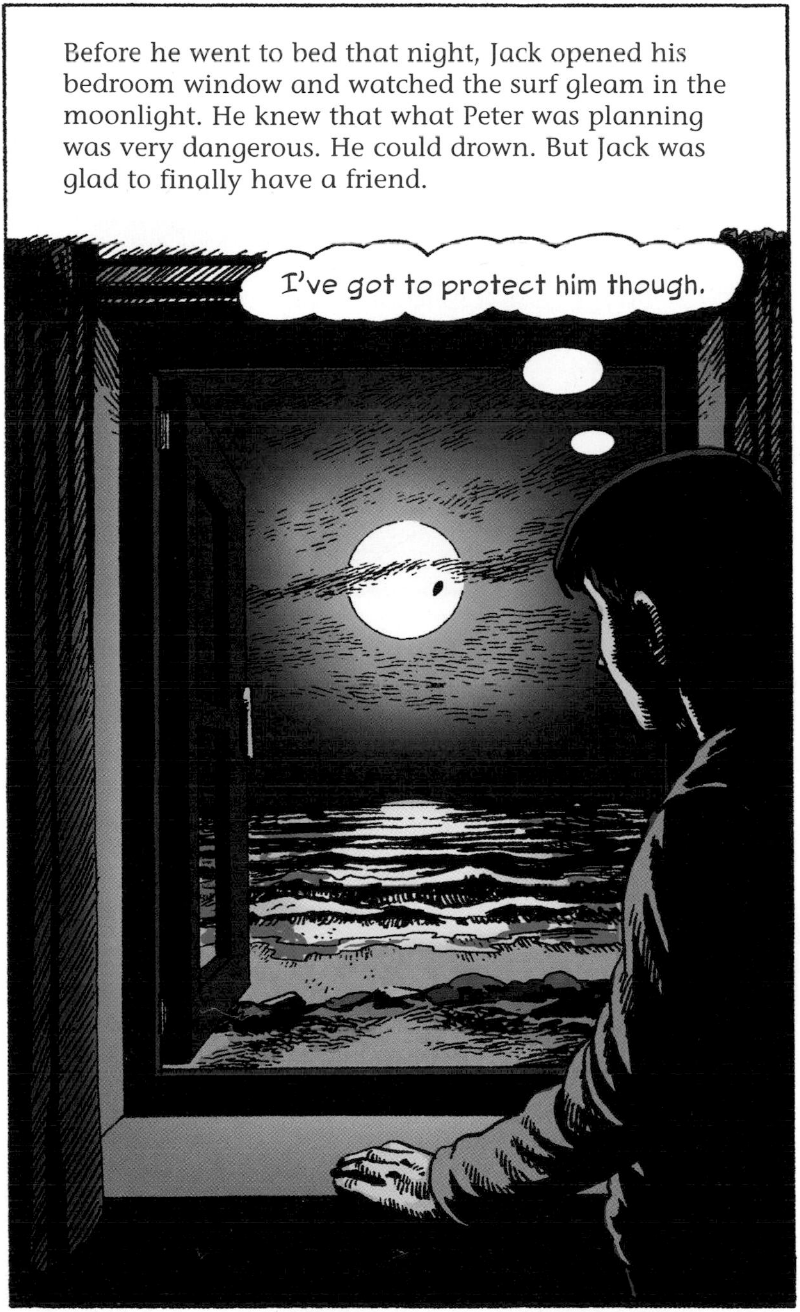
Before he went to bed that night, Jack opened his bedroom window and watched the surf gleam in the moonlight. He knew that what Peter was planning was very dangerous. He could drown. But Jack was glad to finally have a friend.
I've got to protect him though.

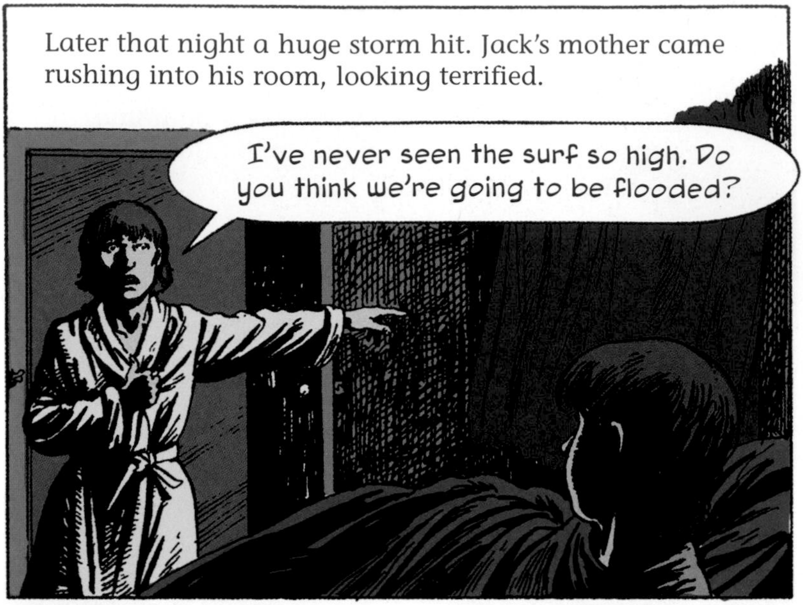
Later that night a huge storm hit. Jack's mother came rushing into his room, looking terrified.
I've never seen the surf so high. Do you think we're going to be flooded?

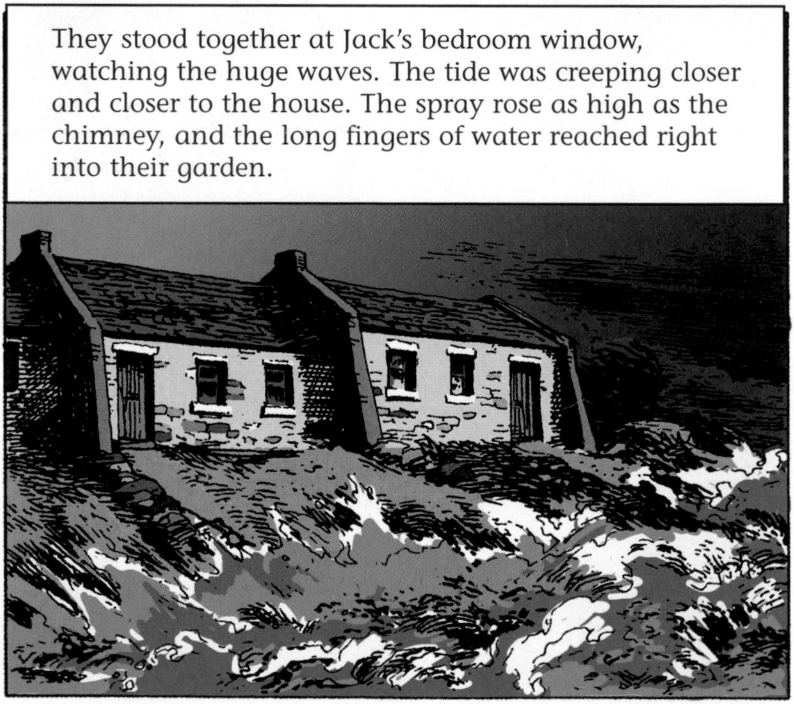
They stood together at Jack's bedroom window, watching the huge waves. The tide was creeping closer and closer to the house. The spray rose as high as the chimney, and the long fingers of water reached right into their garden.

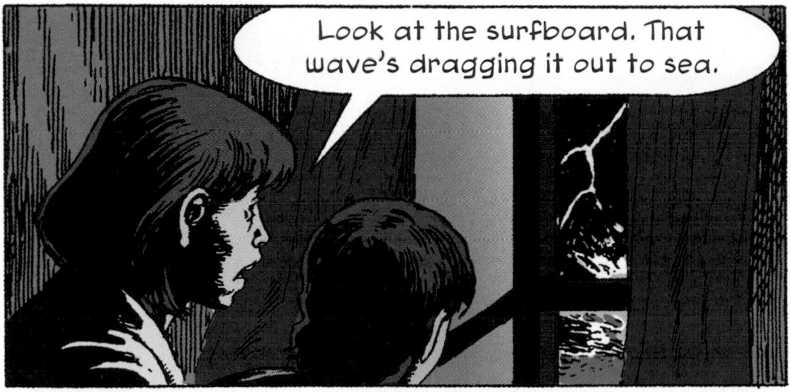
Look at the surfboard. That wave's dragging it out to sea.

Jack gazed over at the next building. Peter had left the surfboard just under the kitchen window, but now it was floating down the garden.

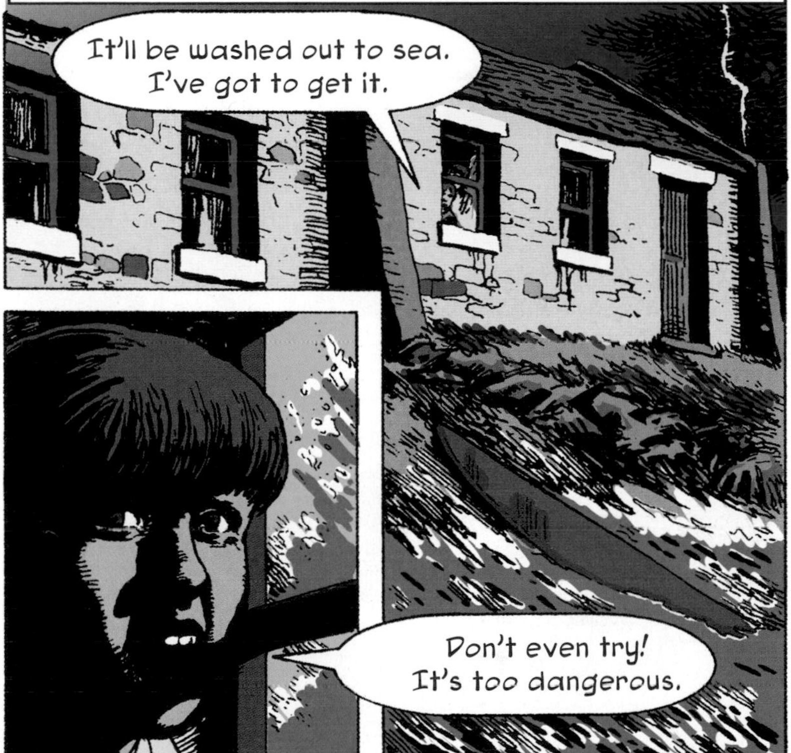
It'll be washed out to sea. I've got to get it.
Don't even try! It's too dangerous.

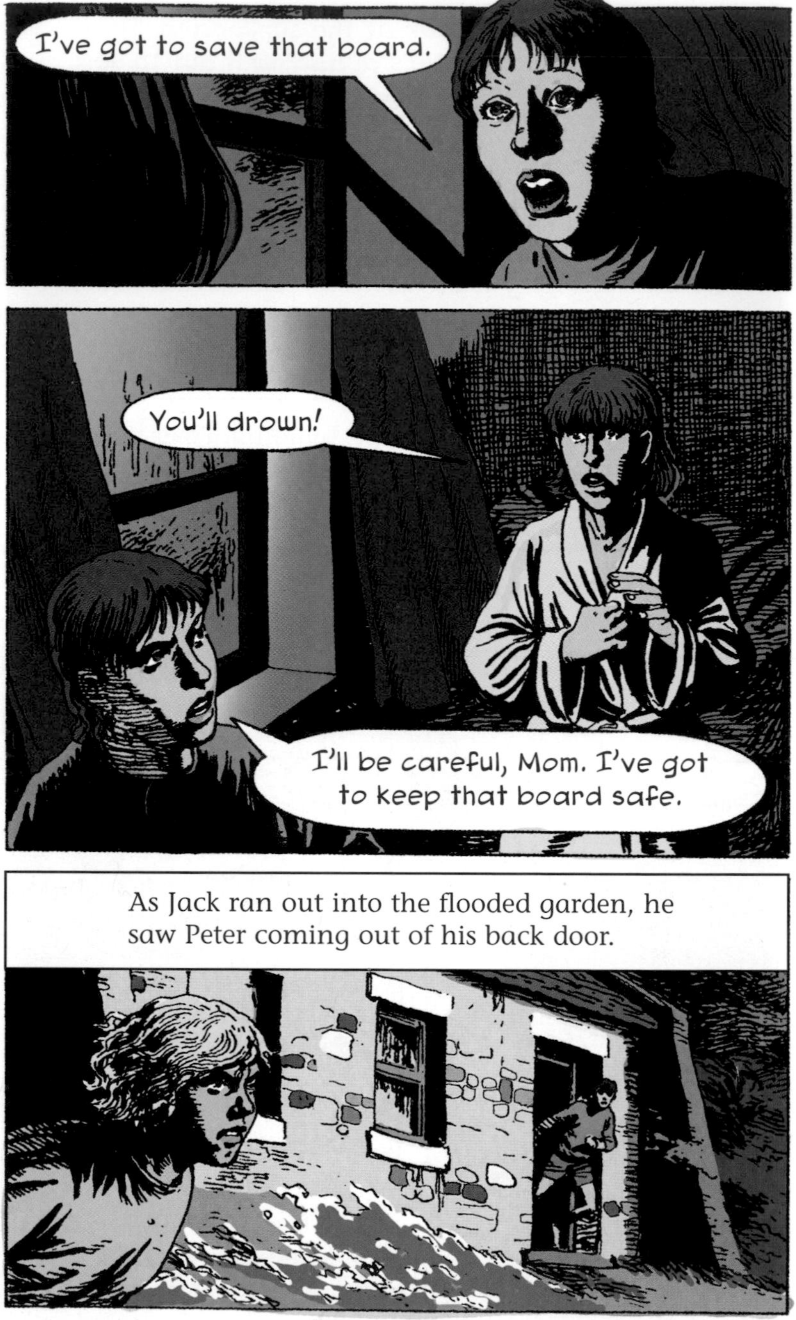
I've got to save that board.
You'll drown!
I'll be careful, Mom. I've got to keep that board safe.
As Jack ran out into the flooded garden, he saw Peter coming out of his back door.

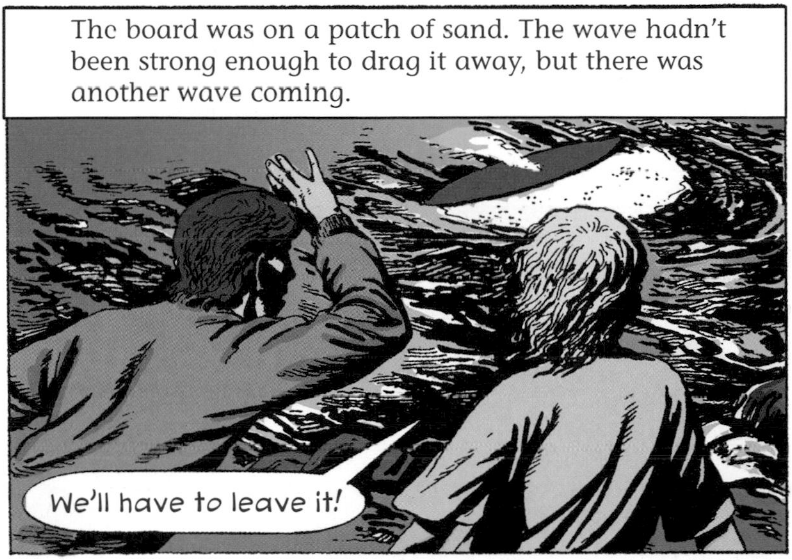
The board was on a patch of sand. The wave hadn't been strong enough to drag it away, but there was another wave coming.
We'll have to leave it!

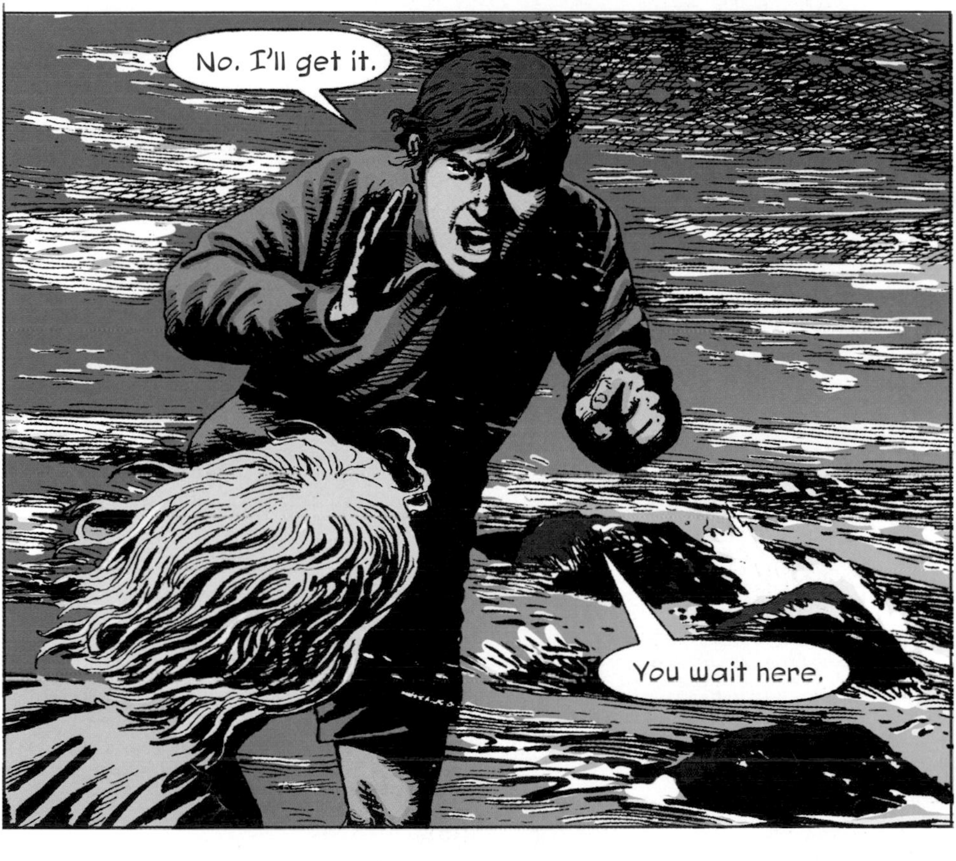
No. I'll get it.
You wait here.

Jack had always been a fast runner. Now he had to be even faster. The next huge wave was rushing toward him.

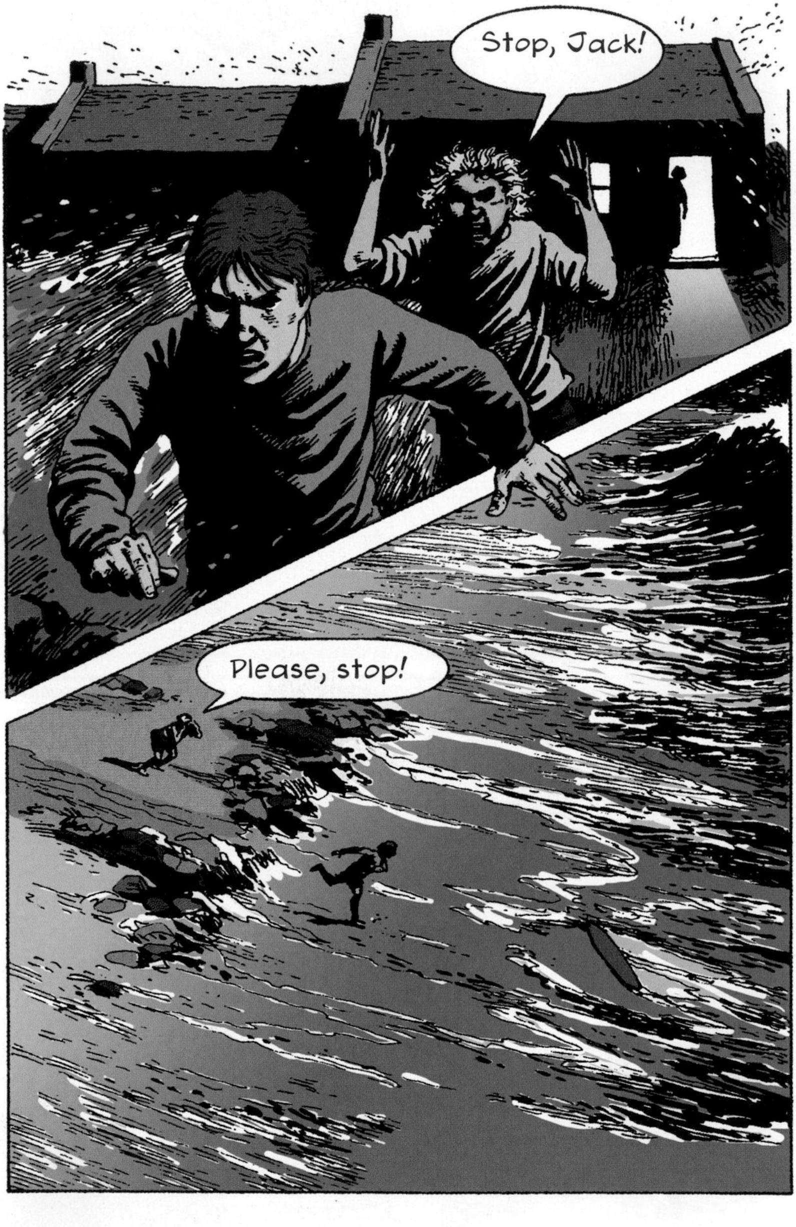
Stop, Jack!
Please, stop!

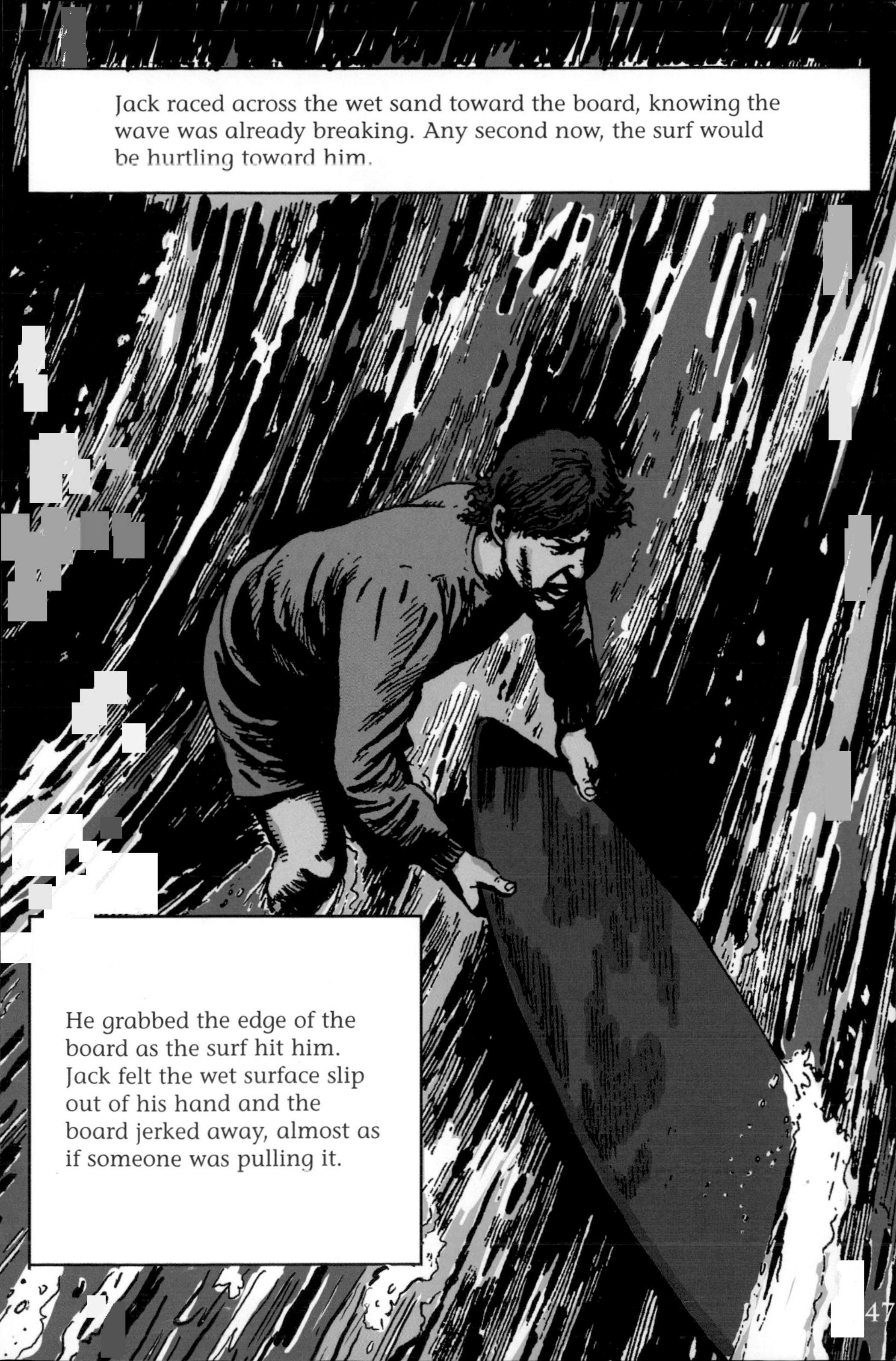
Jack raced across the wet sand toward the board, knowing the wave was already breaking. Any second now, the surf would be hurtling toward him.
He grabbed the edge of the board as the surf hit him. Jack felt the wet surface slip out of his hand and the board jerked away, almost as if someone was pulling it.

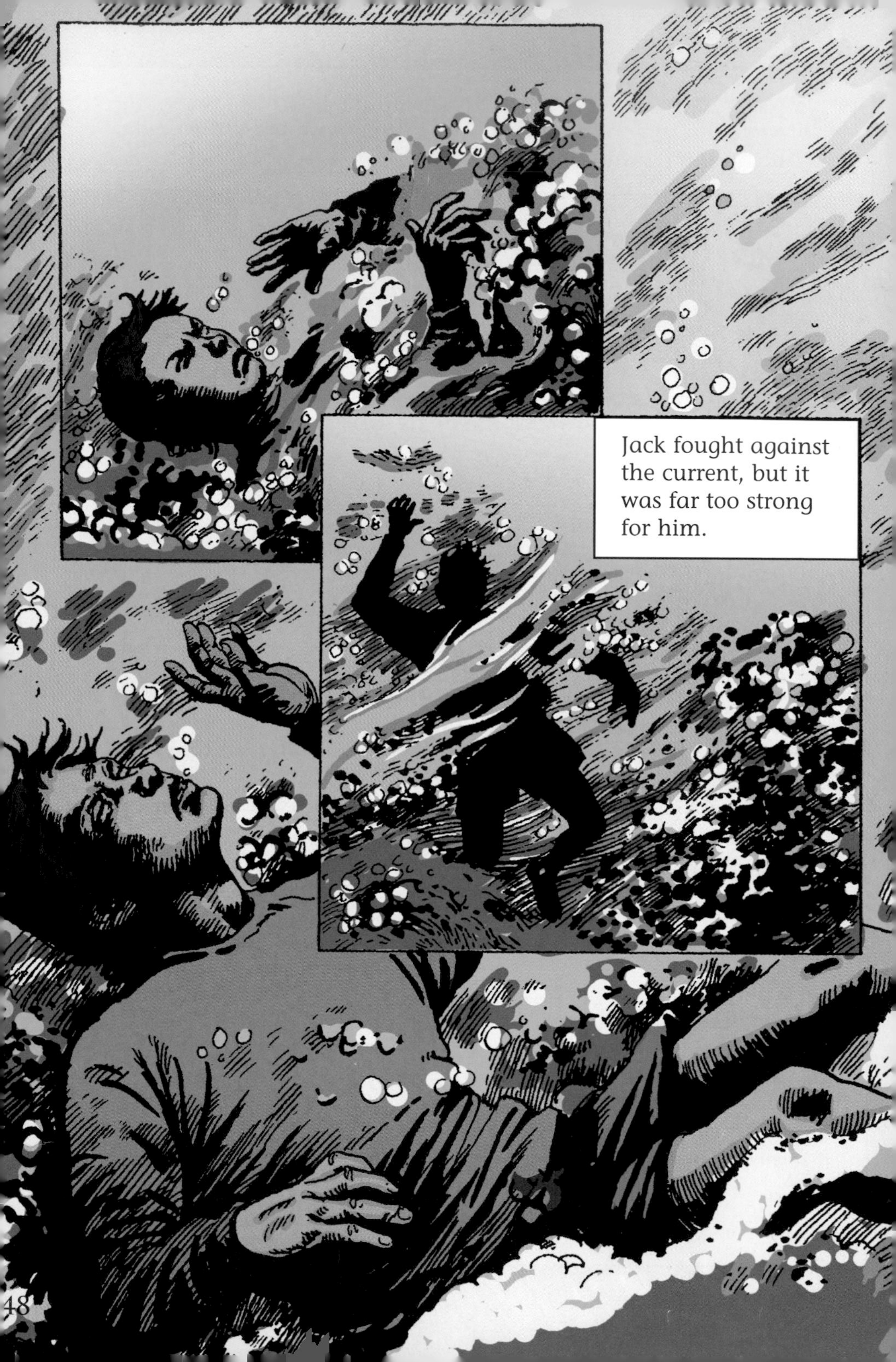
Jack fought against the current, but it was far too strong for him.

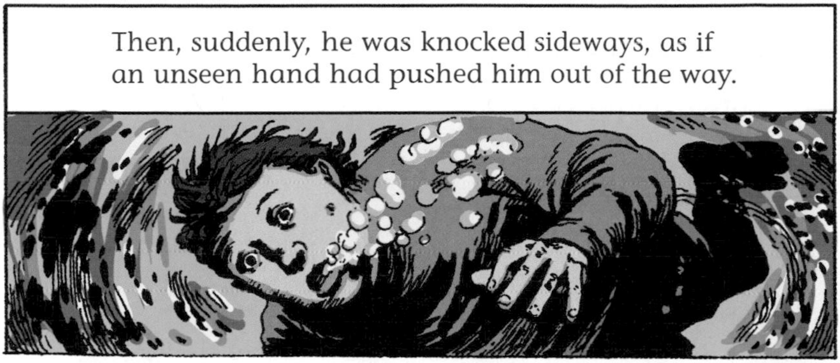
Then, suddenly, he was knocked sideways, as if an unseen hand had pushed him out of the way.

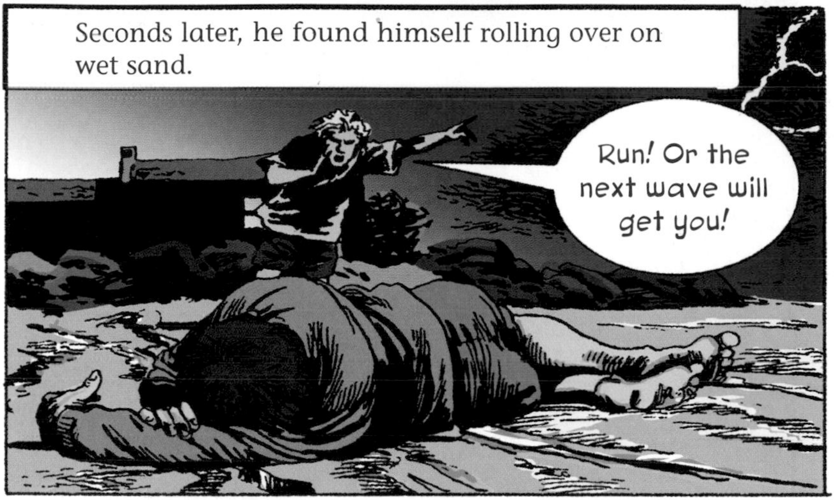
Seconds later, he found himself rolling over on wet sand.
Run! Or the next wave will get you!

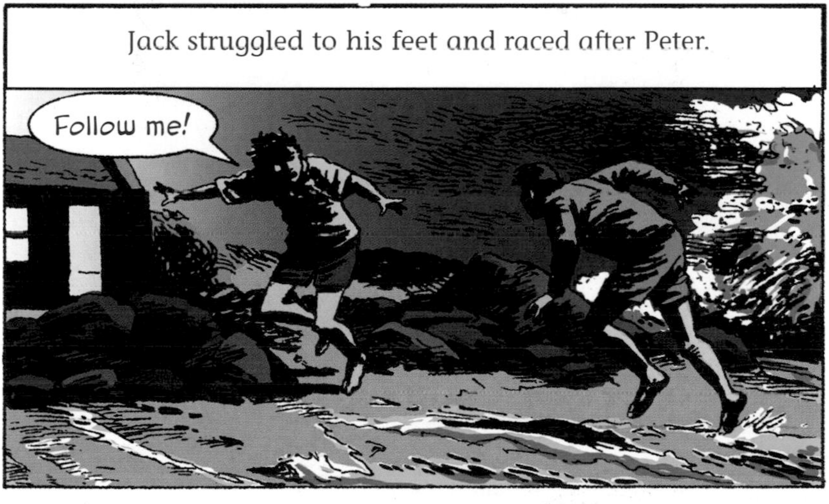
Jack struggled to his feet and raced after Peter.
Follow me!

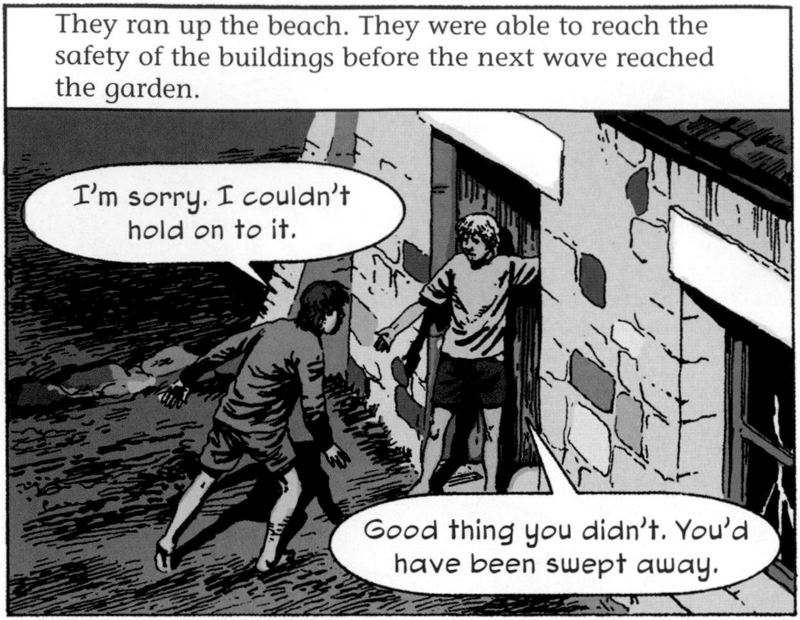
They ran up the beach. They were able to reach the safety of the buildings before the next wave reached the garden.
I'm sorry. I couldn't hold on to it.
Good thing you didn't. You'd have been swept away.

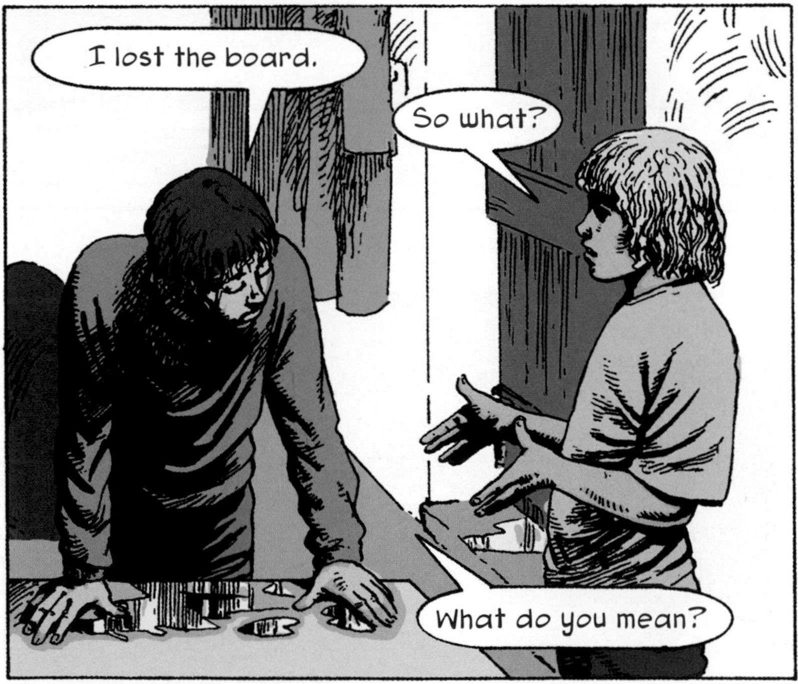
I lost the board.
So what?
What do you mean?

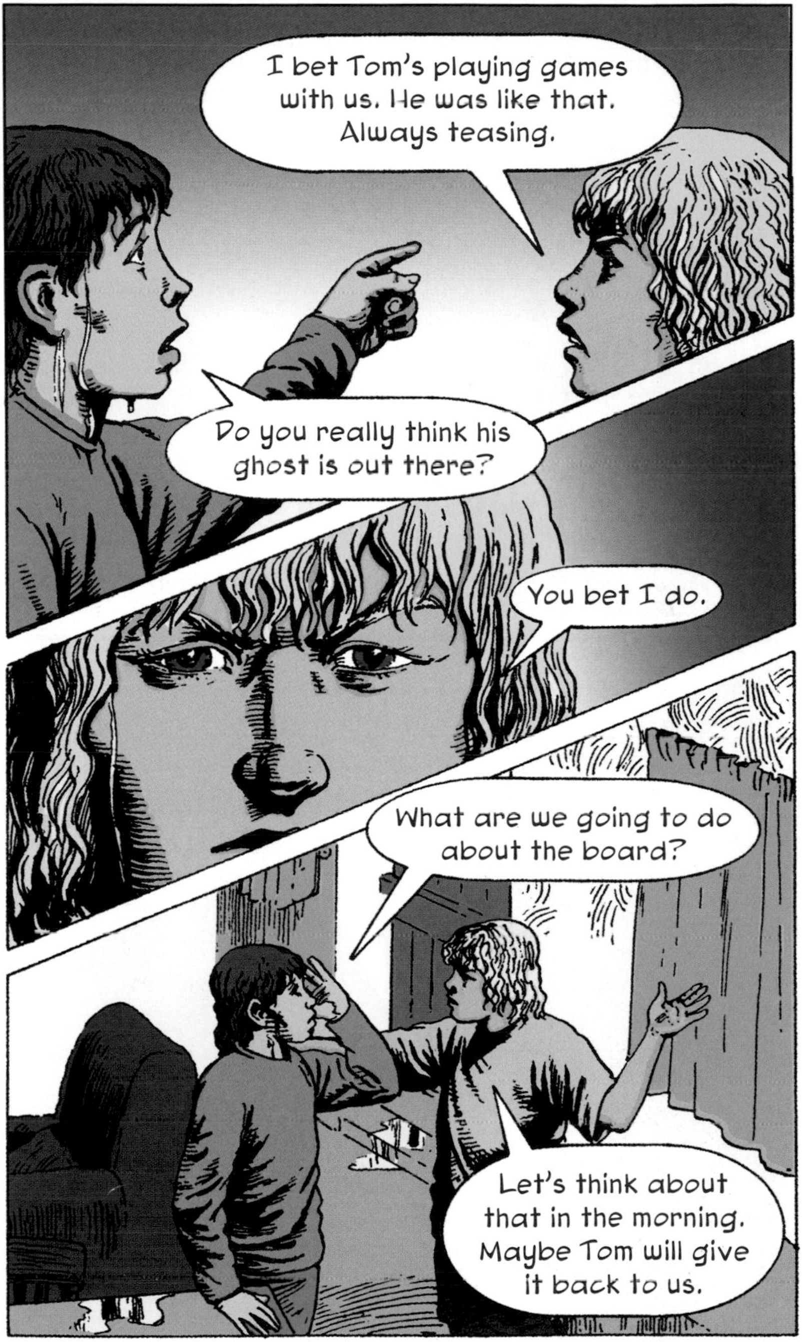
I bet Tom's playing games with us. He was like that. Always teasing.
Do you really think his ghost is out there?
You bet I do.
What are we going to do about the board?
Let's think about that in the morning. Maybe Tom will give it back to us.

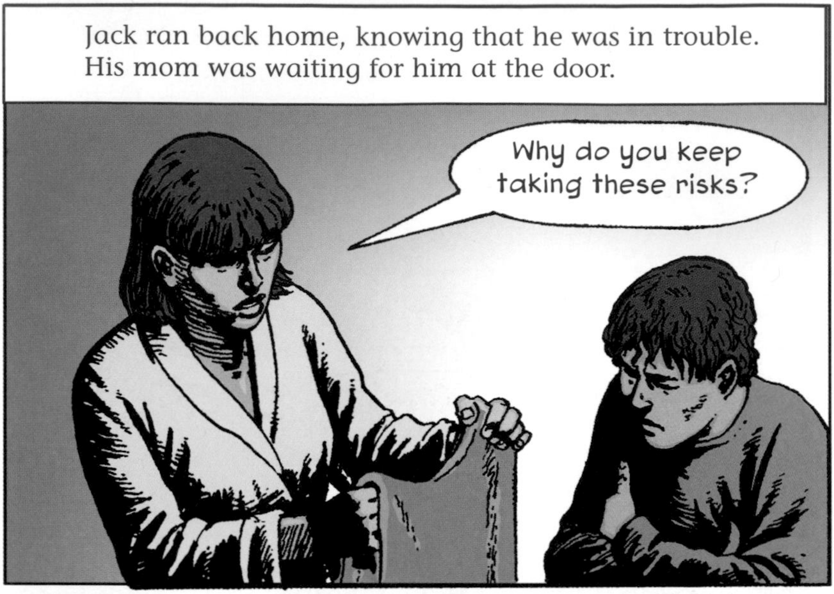
Jack ran back home, knowing that he was in trouble. His mom was waiting for him at the door.
Why do you keep taking these risks?

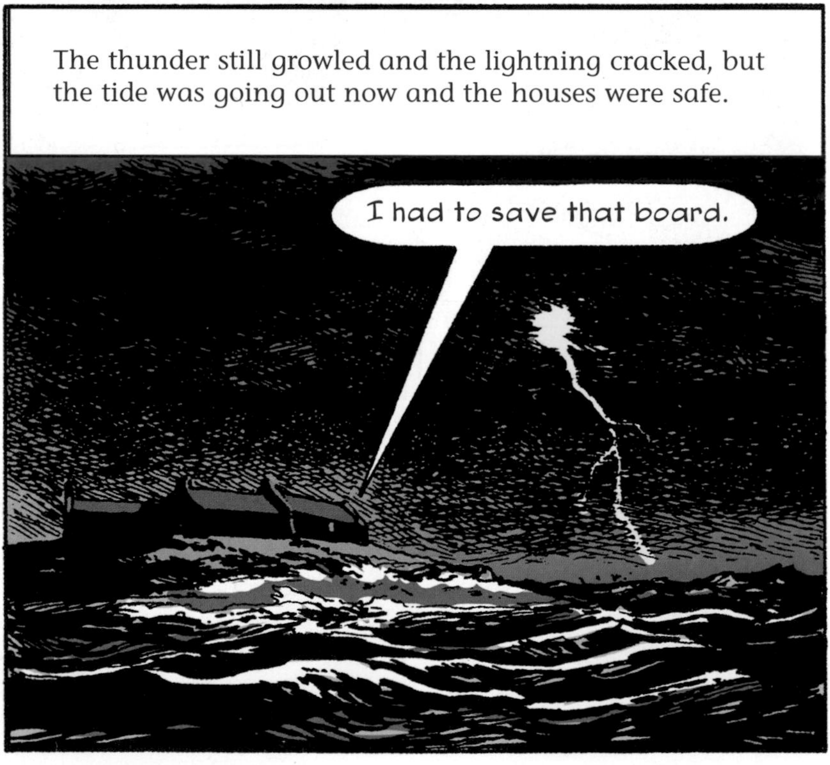
The thunder still growled and the lightning cracked, but the tide was going out now and the houses were safe.
I had to save that board.

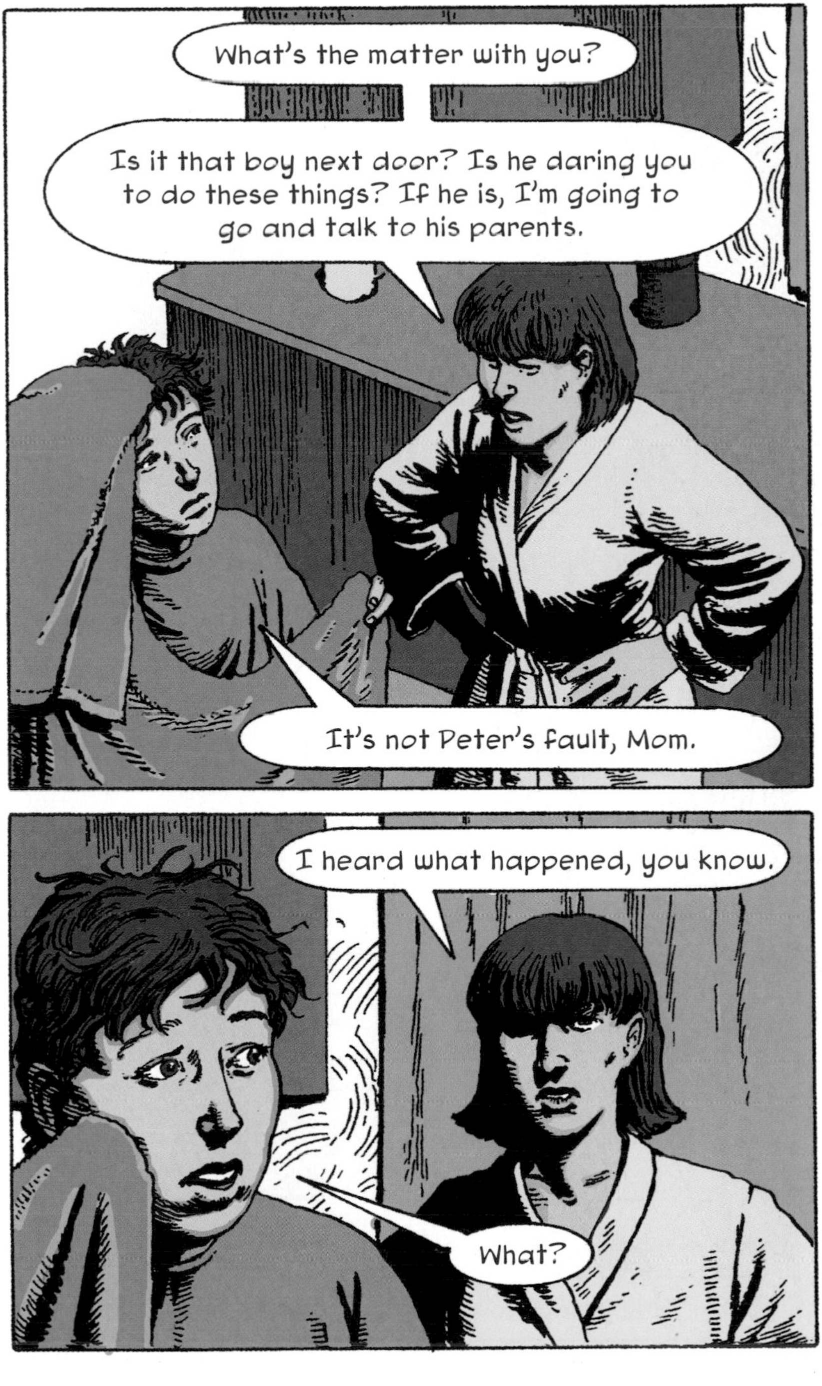
What's the matter with you?
Is it that boy next door? Is he daring you to do these things? If he is, I'm going to go and talk to his parents.
It's not Peter's fault, Mom.
I heard what happened, you know.
What?

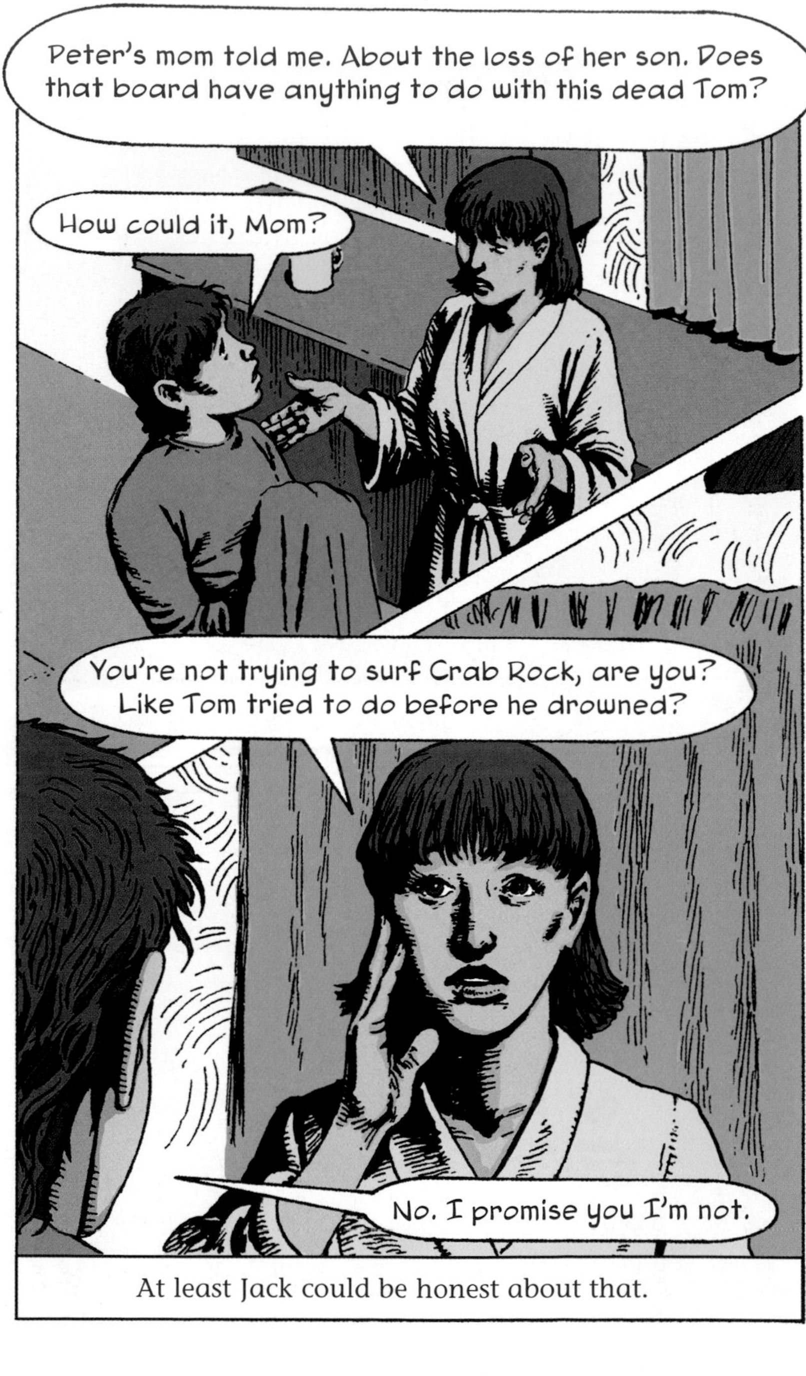
Peter's mom told me. About the loss of her son. Does that board have anything to do with this dead Tom?
How could it, Mom?
You're not trying to surf Crab Rock, are you? Like Tom tried to do before he drowned?
No. I promise you I'm not.

At least Jack could be honest about that.

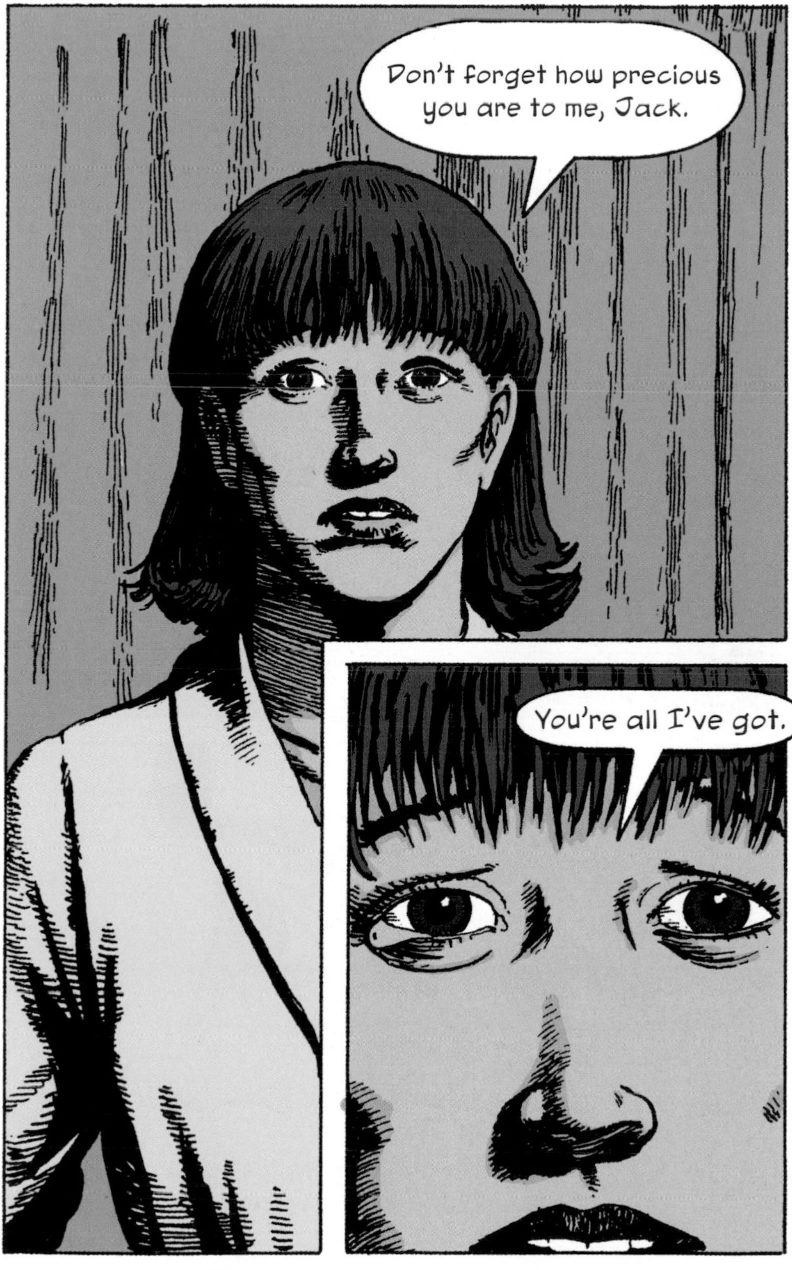
Don't forget how precious you are to me, Jack.
You're all I've got.

CHAPTER FIVE

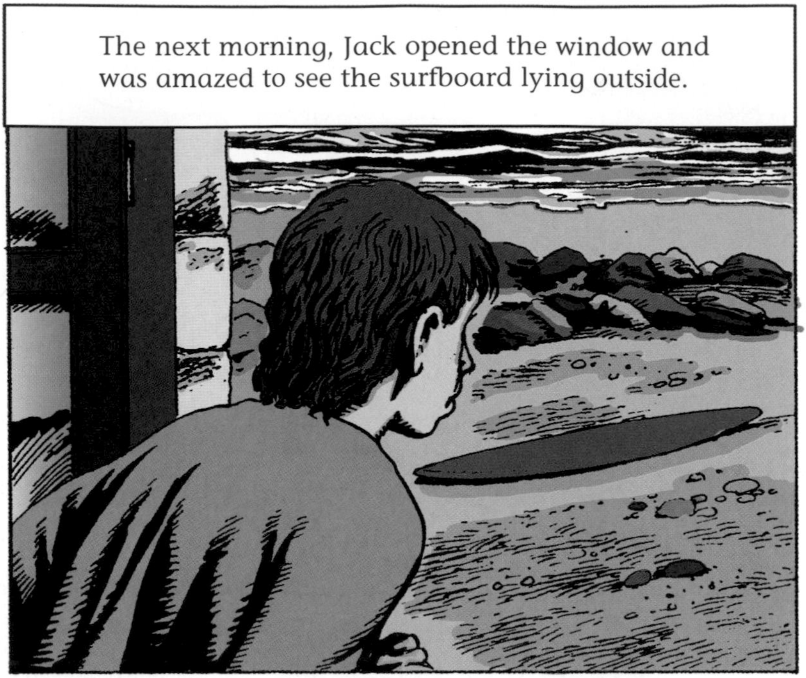
The next morning, Jack opened the window and was amazed to see the surfboard lying outside.

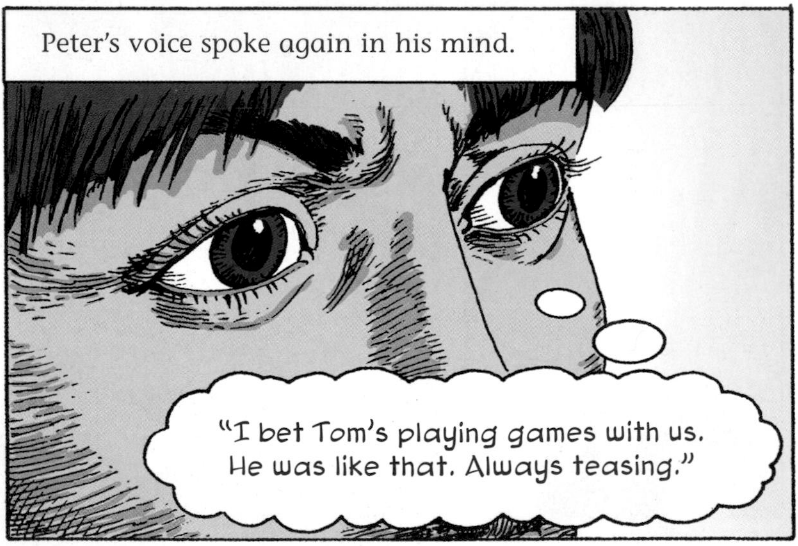
Peter's voice spoke again in his mind.
"I bet Tom's playing games with us. He was like that. Always teasing."

Jack cautiously opened the front door. As he grabbed the board it seemed to move in his hands. Maybe Tom was just playing games.

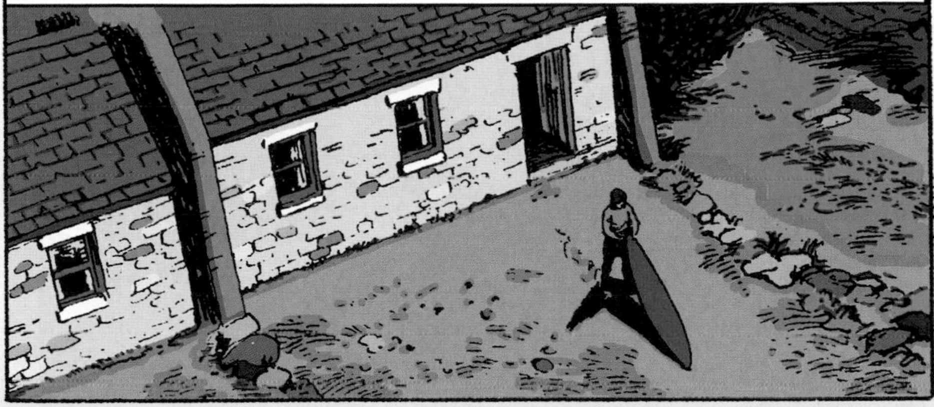

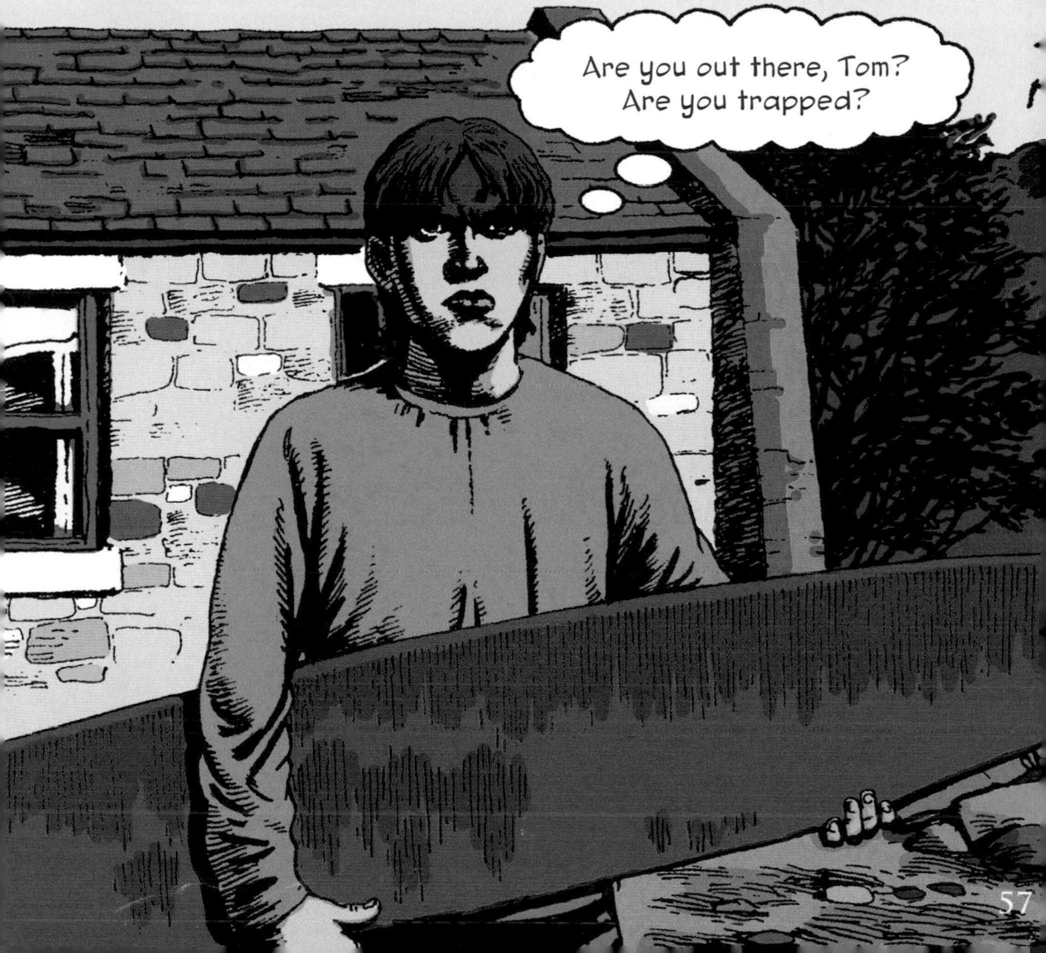
Are you out there, Tom? Are you trapped?

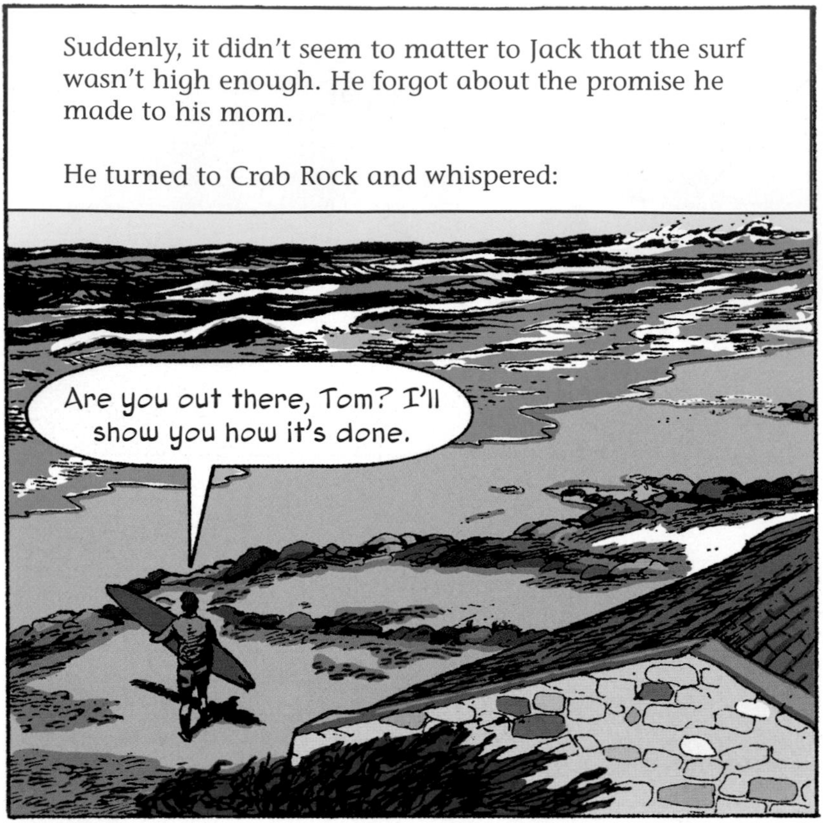
Suddenly, it didn't seem to matter to Jack that the surf wasn't high enough. He forgot about the promise he made to his mom.
He turned to Crab Rock and whispered:
Are you out there, Tom? I'll show you how it's done.

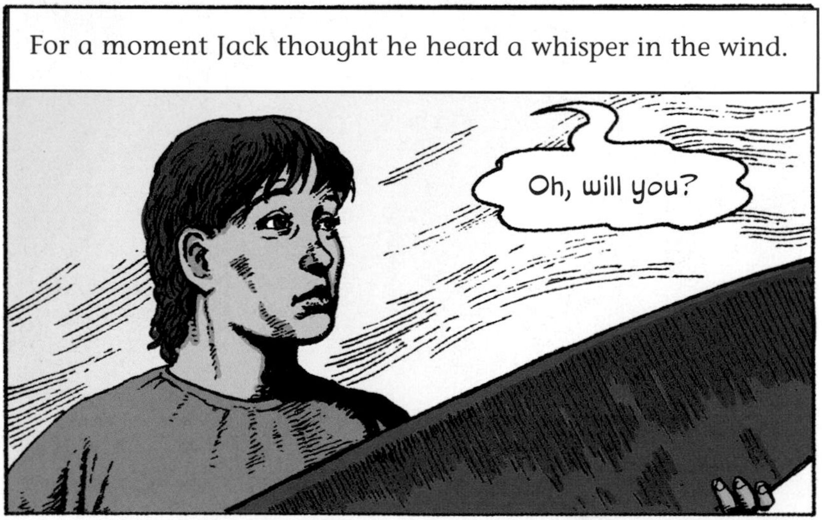
For a moment Jack thought he heard a whisper in the wind.
Oh, will you?

Hoping his mother was still asleep, Jack put on his wetsuit, picked up the surfboard, and ran down the beach toward the surf.

Seconds later he heard feet pounding on the sand behind him.

Where do you think you're going?

I thought I'd try the rock.

That's **my** job.

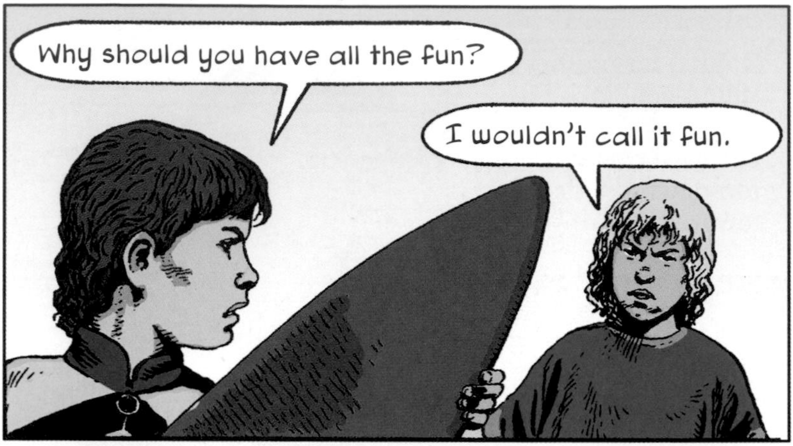
Why should you have all the fun?
I wouldn't call it fun.

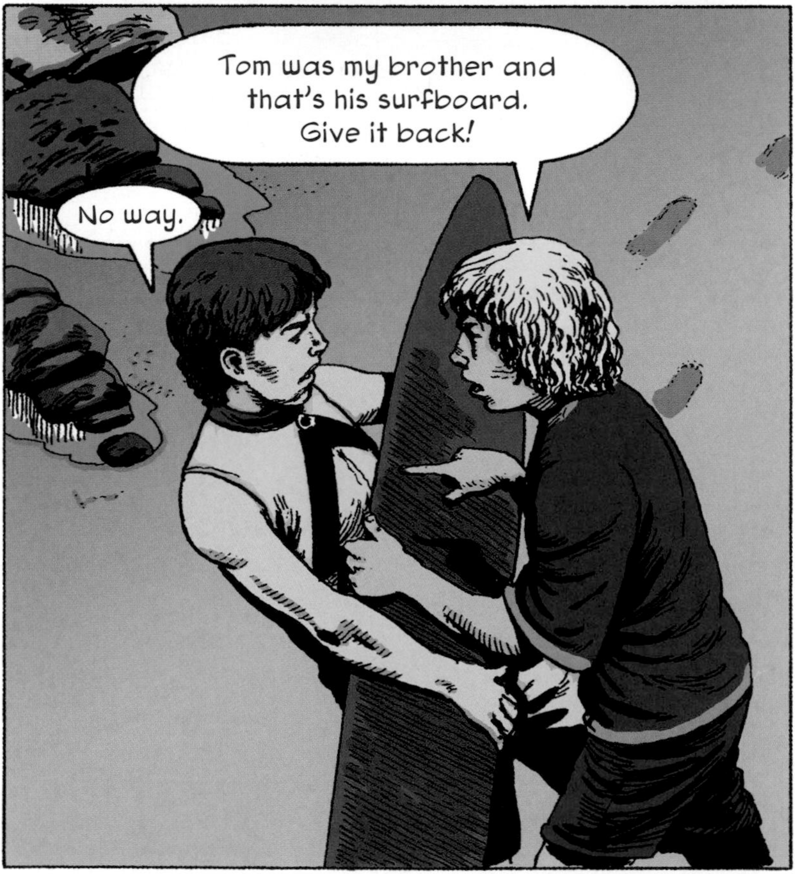
Tom was my brother and that's his surfboard. Give it back!
No way.

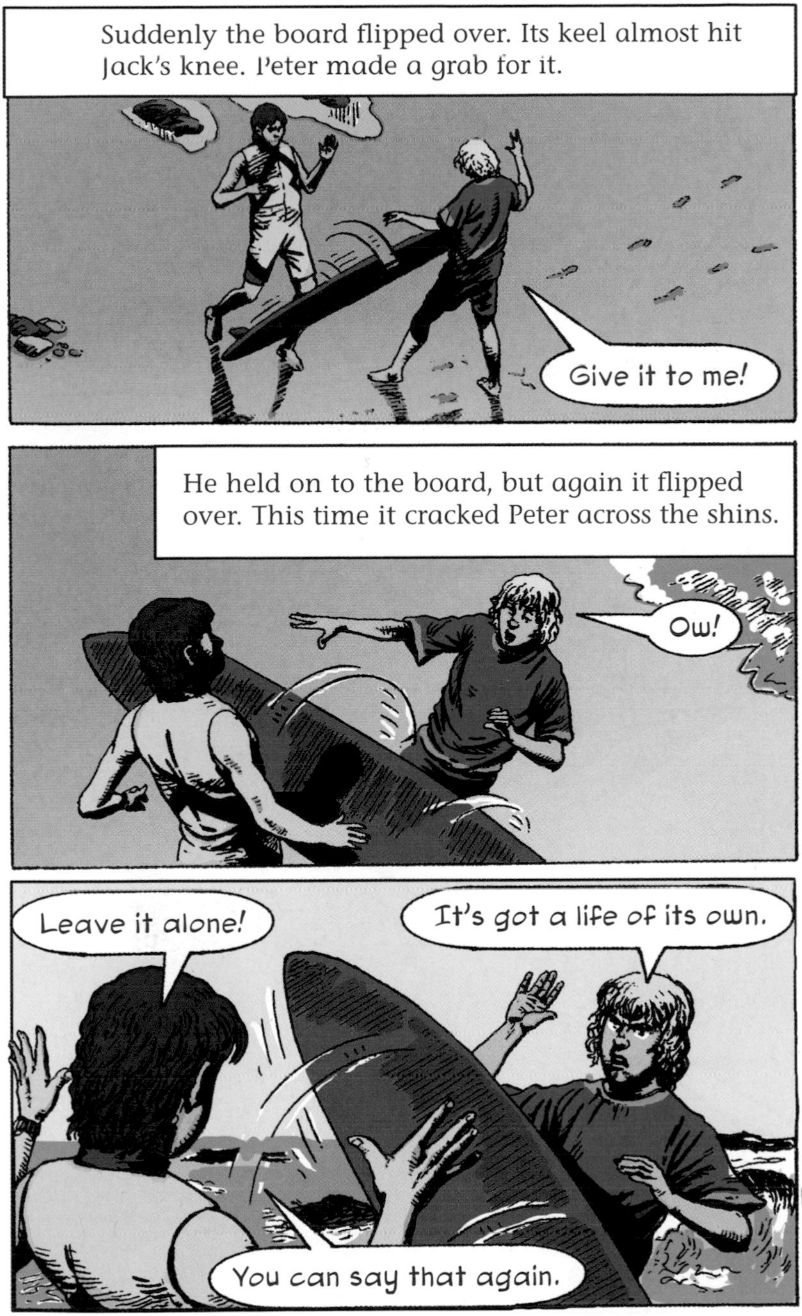
Suddenly the board flipped over. Its keel almost hit Jack's knee. Peter made a grab for it.
Give it to me!
He held on to the board, but again it flipped over. This time it cracked Peter across the shins.
Ow!
Leave it alone!
It's got a life of its own.
You can say that again.

The board lay on the sand between them. With a sudden lunge, Peter made another grab for it and then backed off with a sharp cry.

What happened?

It gave me a splinter!

Let me see it.

Peter howled in pain as Jack pulled it out.

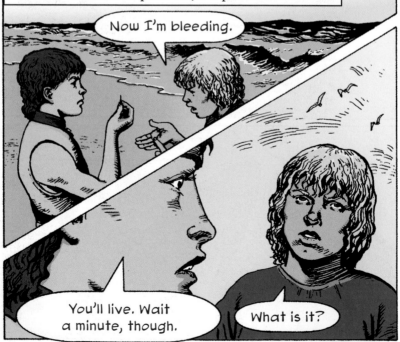

Now I'm bleeding.

You'll live. Wait a minute, though.

What is it?

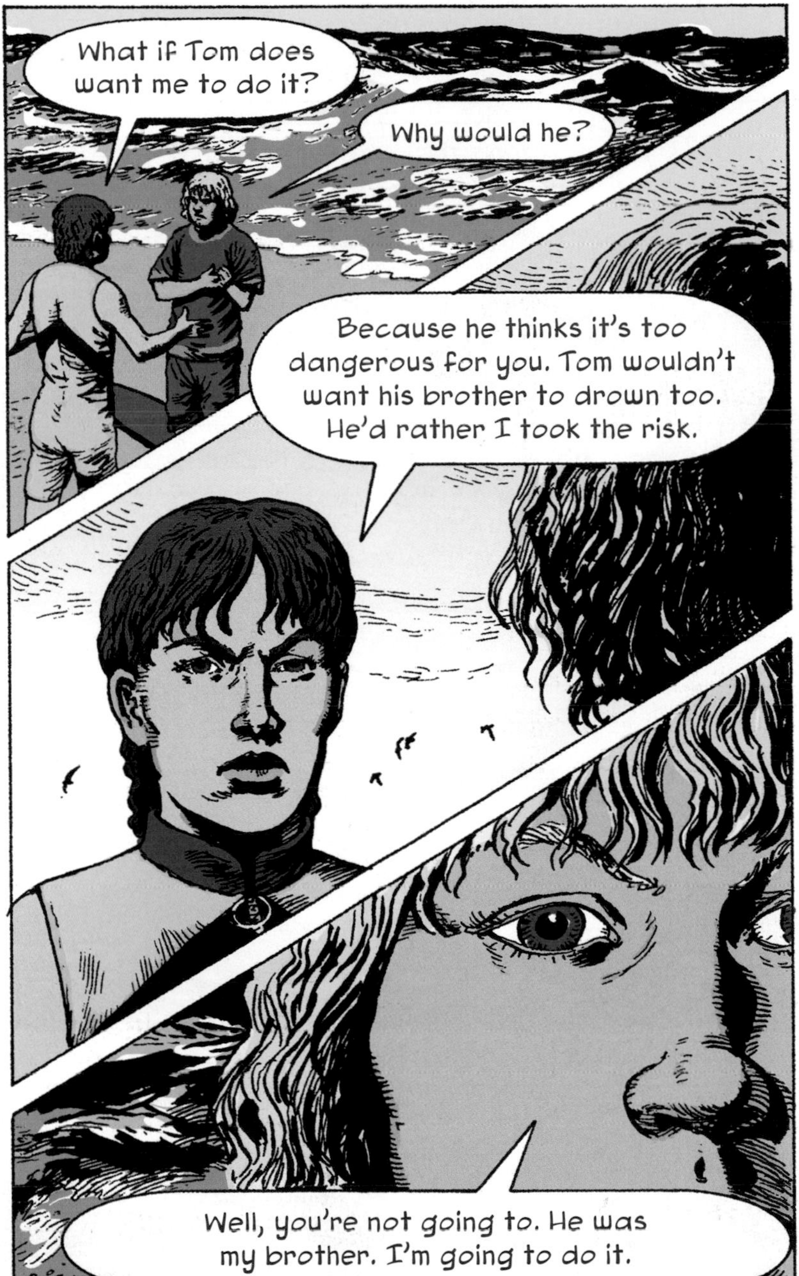
What if Tom does want me to do it?
Why would he?
Because he thinks it's too dangerous for you. Tom wouldn't want his brother to drown too. He'd rather I took the risk.
Well, you're not going to. He was my brother. I'm going to do it.

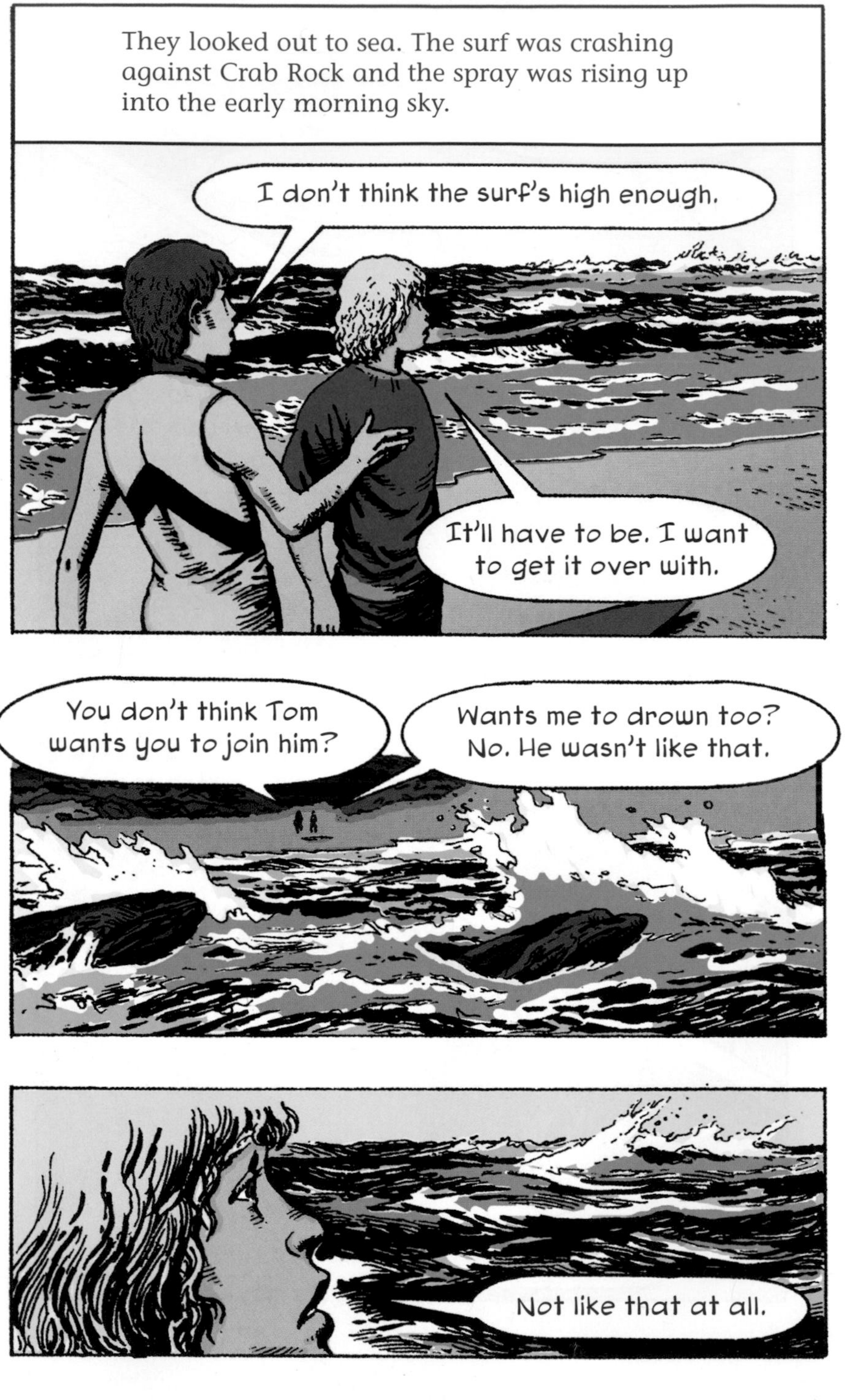
They looked out to sea. The surf was crashing against Crab Rock and the spray was rising up into the early morning sky.
I don't think the surf's high enough.
It'll have to be. I want to get it over with.
You don't think Tom wants you to join him?
Wants me to drown too? No. He wasn't like that.
Not like that at all.

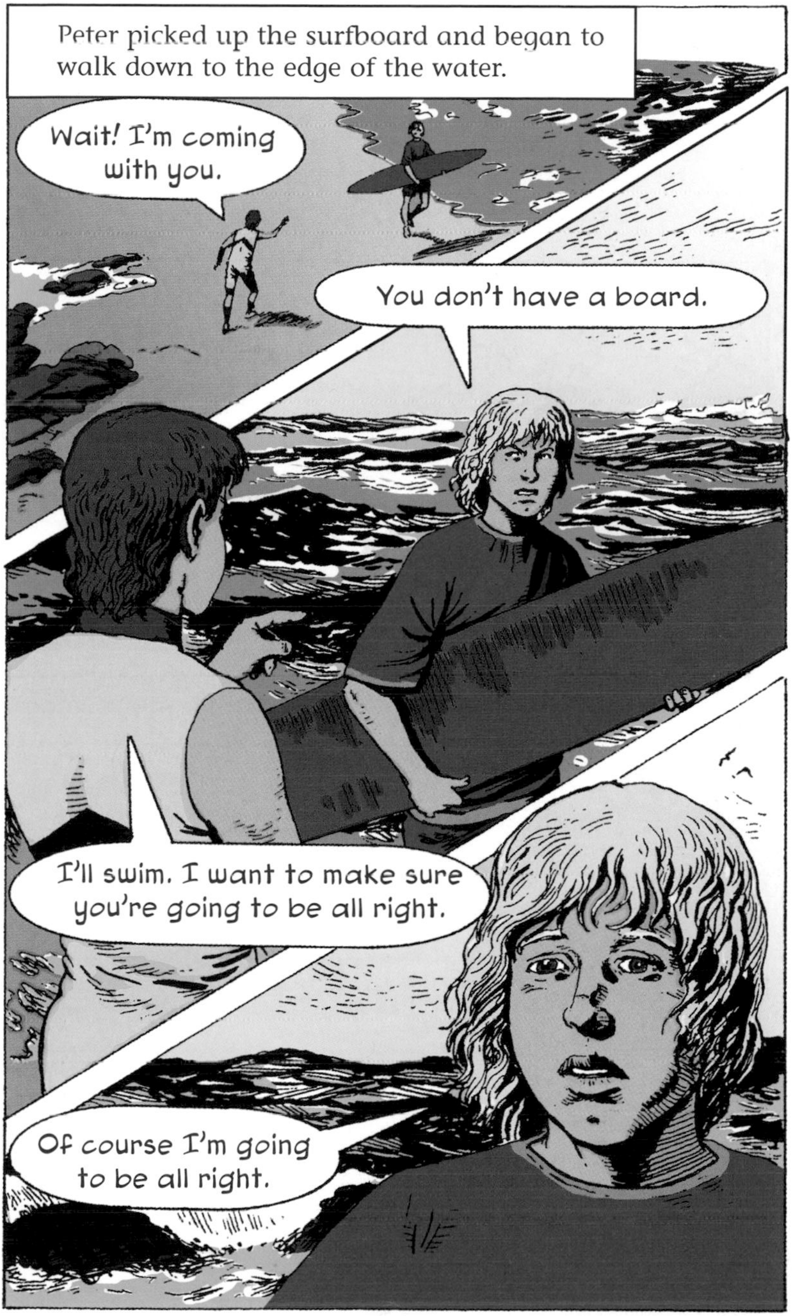
Peter picked up the surfboard and began to walk down to the edge of the water.
Wait! I'm coming with you.
You don't have a board.
I'll swim. I want to make sure you're going to be all right.
Of course I'm going to be all right.

CHAPTER SIX

As Peter paddled out into the surf with Jack
swimming behind him, the sun came out, turning
the waves gold. Peter steered close to Crab Rock,
and waited for a wave of the right height.

Jack watched him from a safe distance.

He's having to wait a long time.
None of the waves are big enough.

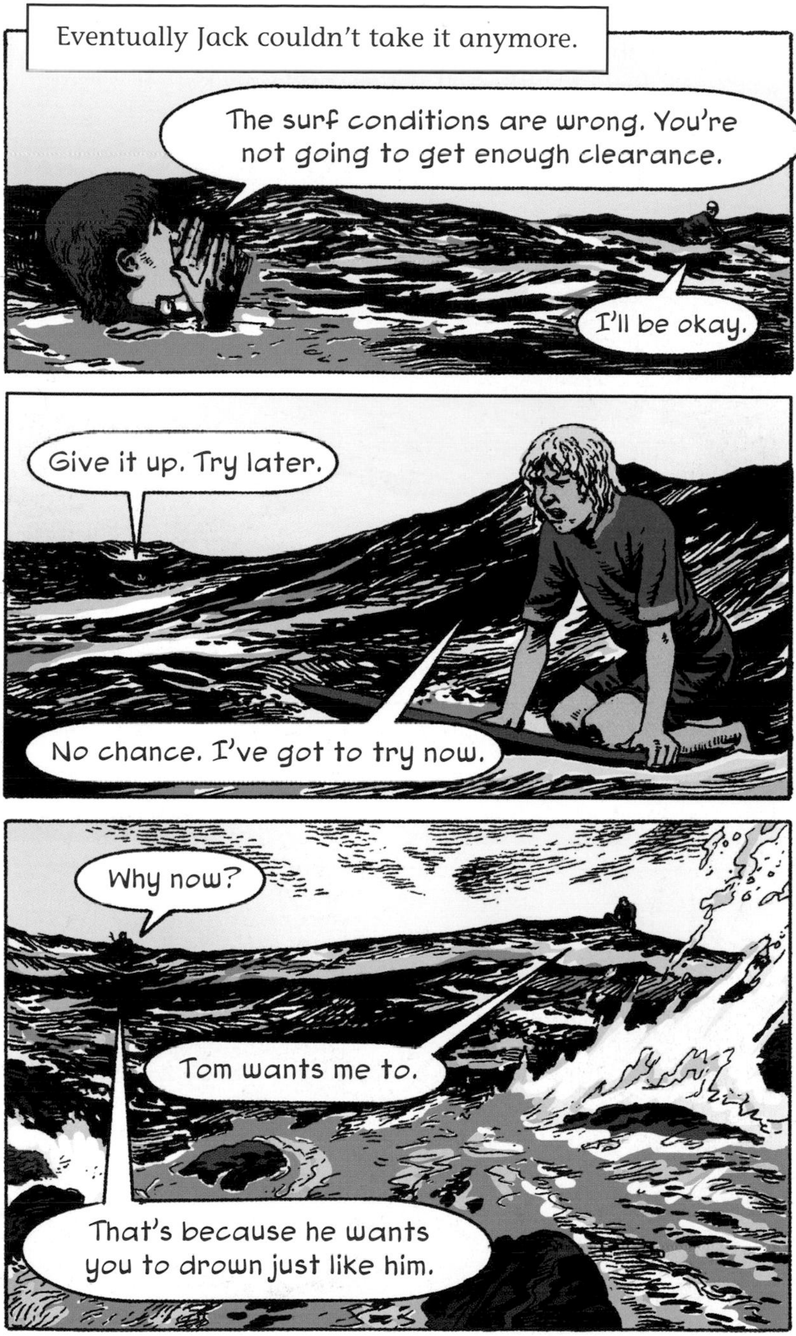
Eventually Jack couldn't take it anymore.
The surf conditions are wrong. You're not going to get enough clearance.
I'll be okay.
Give it up. Try later.
No chance. I've got to try now.
Why now?
Tom wants me to.
That's because he wants you to drown just like him.

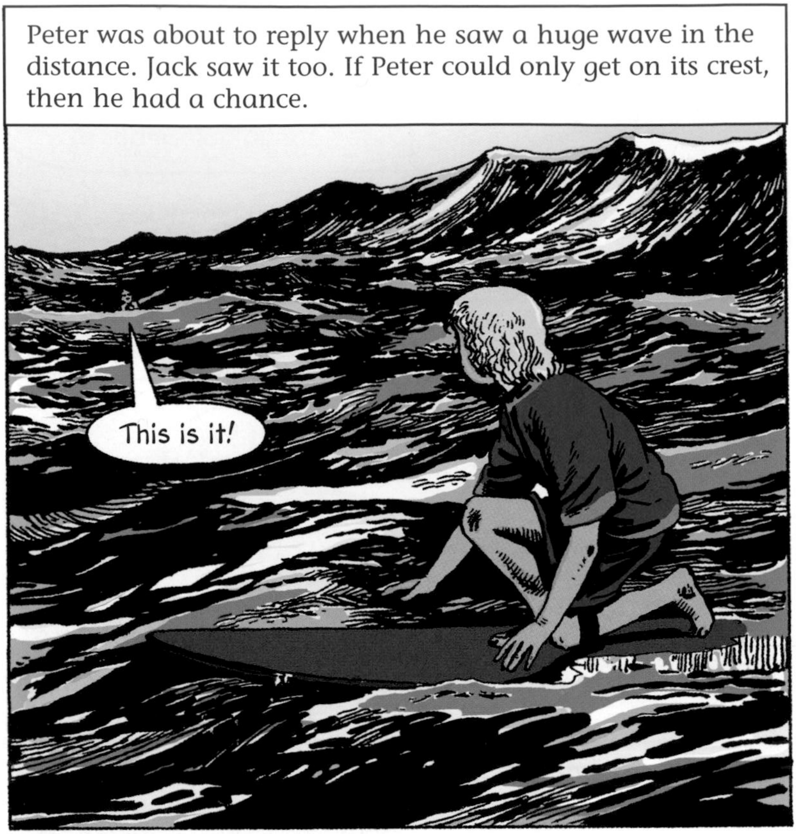
Peter was about to reply when he saw a huge wave in the distance. Jack saw it too. If Peter could only get on its crest, then he had a chance.
This is it!

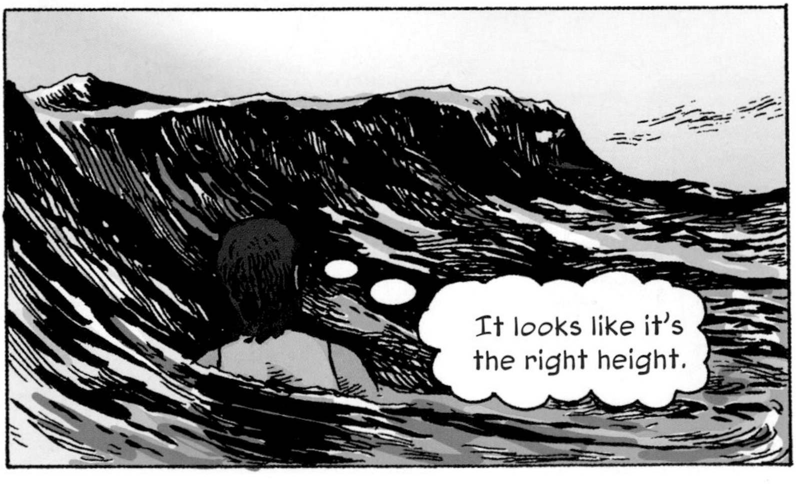
It looks like it's the right height.

Then, at just the right moment, Peter caught the wave and was up on his feet. Jack could hardly believe his eyes as the crest soared above Crab Rock with Peter balancing on Tom's board.

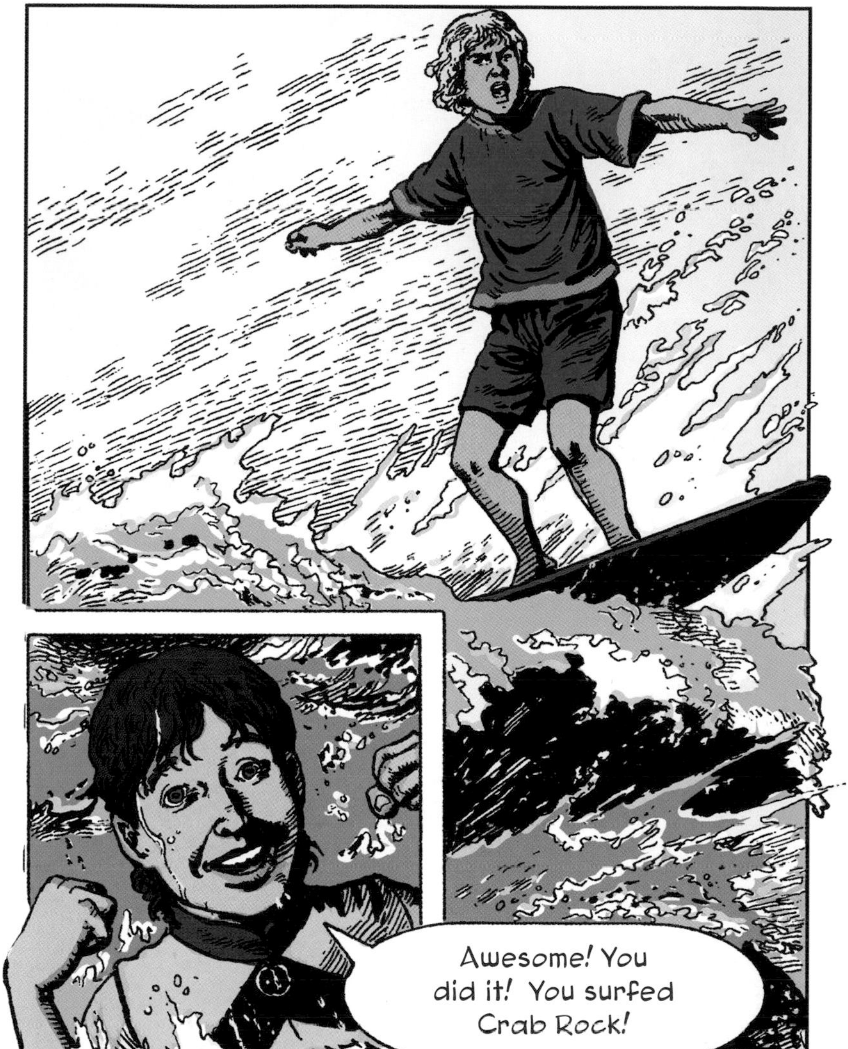
Awesome! You did it! You surfed Crab Rock!

Peter was gliding toward the shore, still on the wave, cheering and clapping. Then, for no reason, he fell off his board. To Jack, it looked as if someone had pushed him.

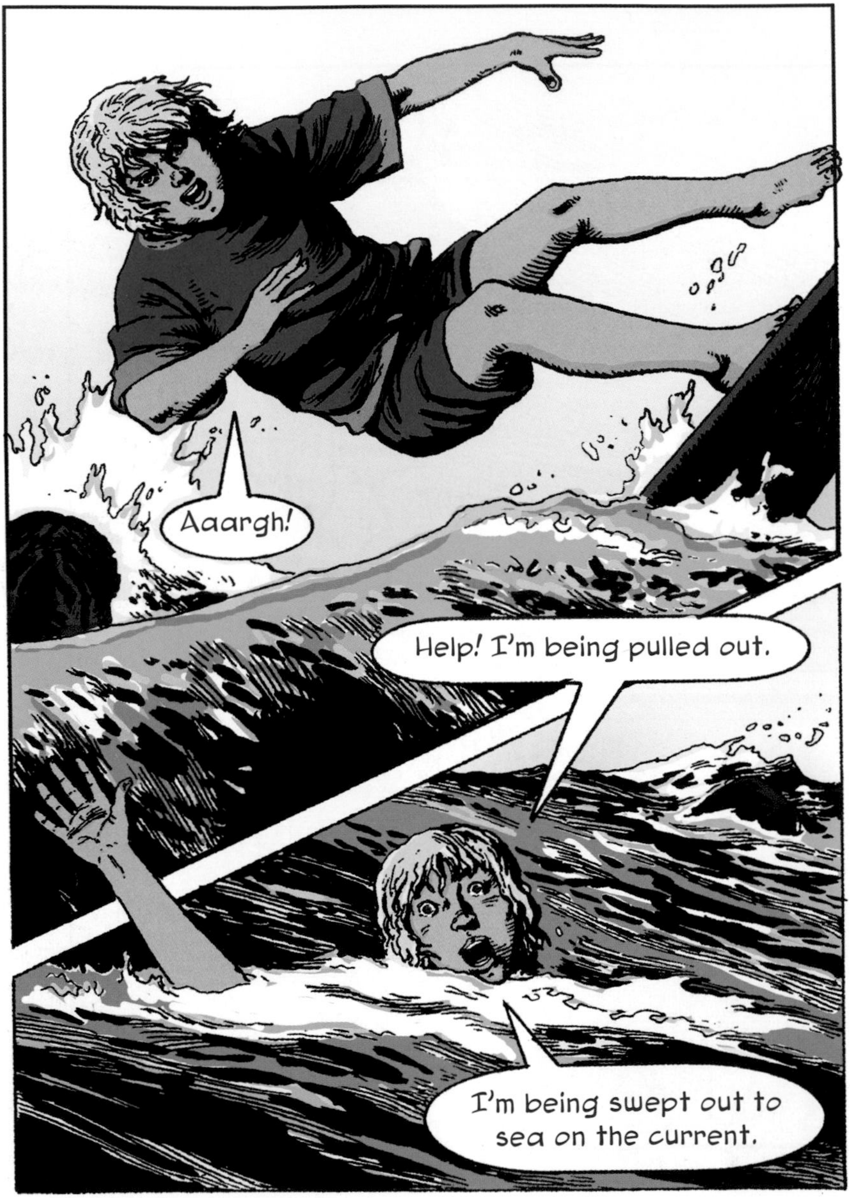
Aaargh!
Help! I'm being pulled out.
I'm being swept out to sea on the current.

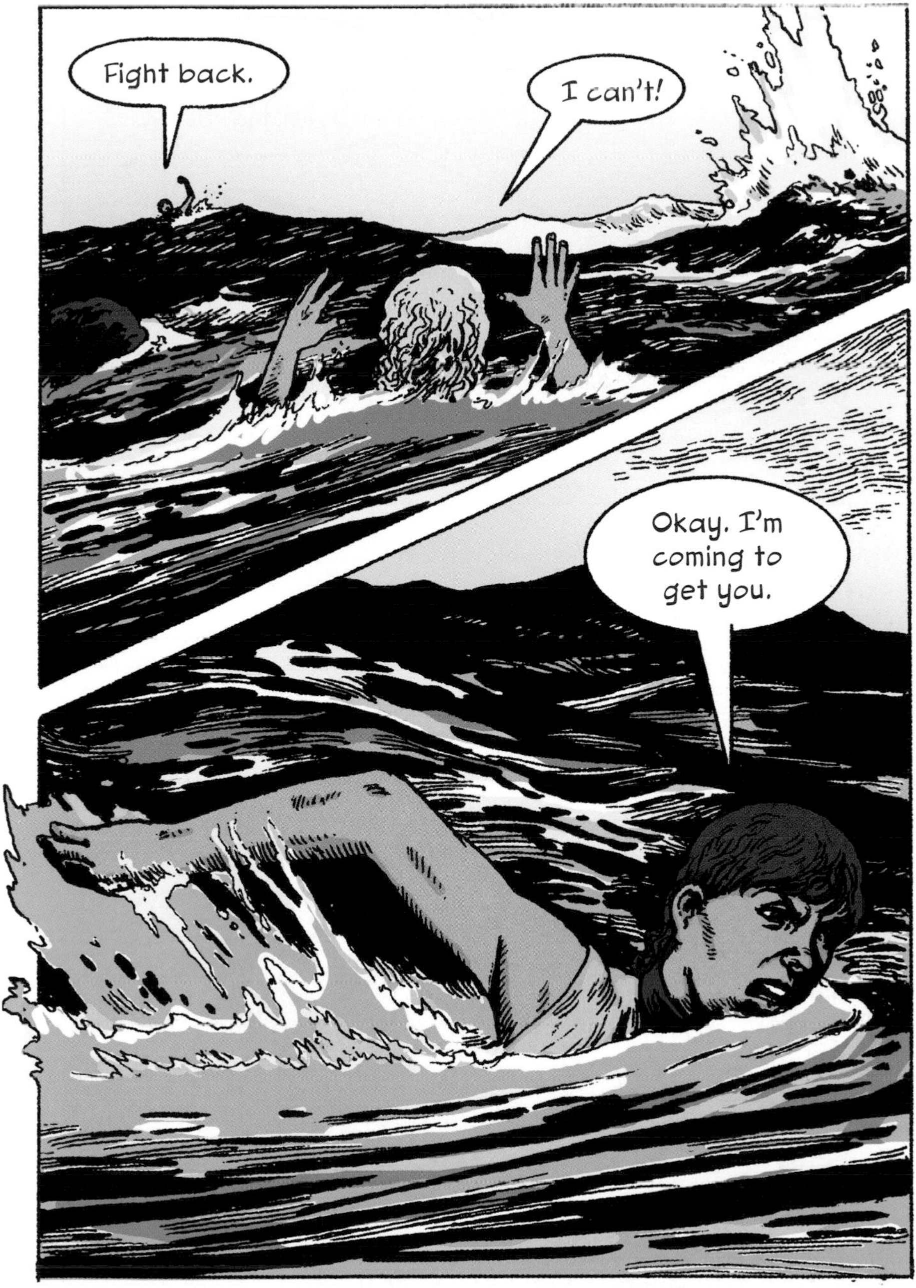
Fight back.
I can't!
Okay. I'm coming to get you.

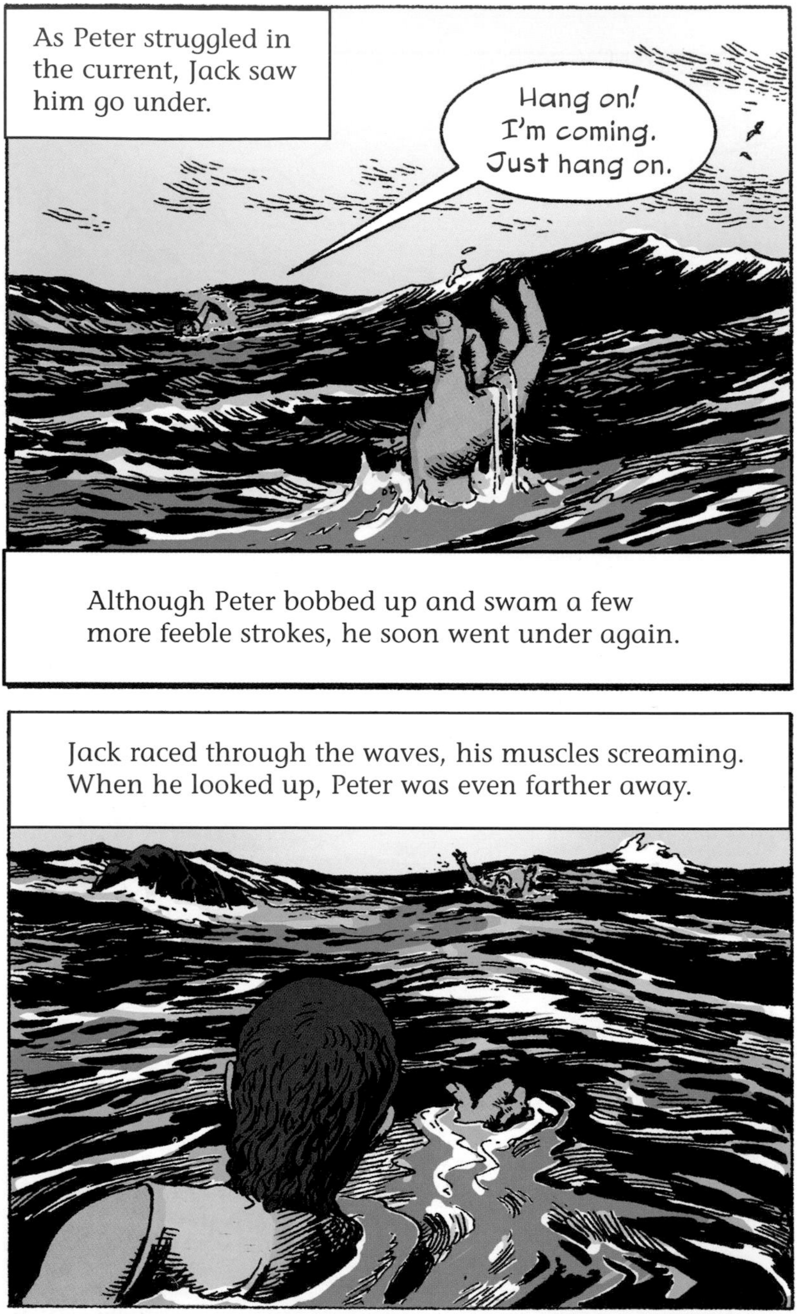
As Peter struggled in the current, Jack saw him go under.
Hang on! I'm coming. Just hang on.
Although Peter bobbed up and swam a few more feeble strokes, he soon went under again.
Jack raced through the waves, his muscles screaming. When he looked up, Peter was even farther away.

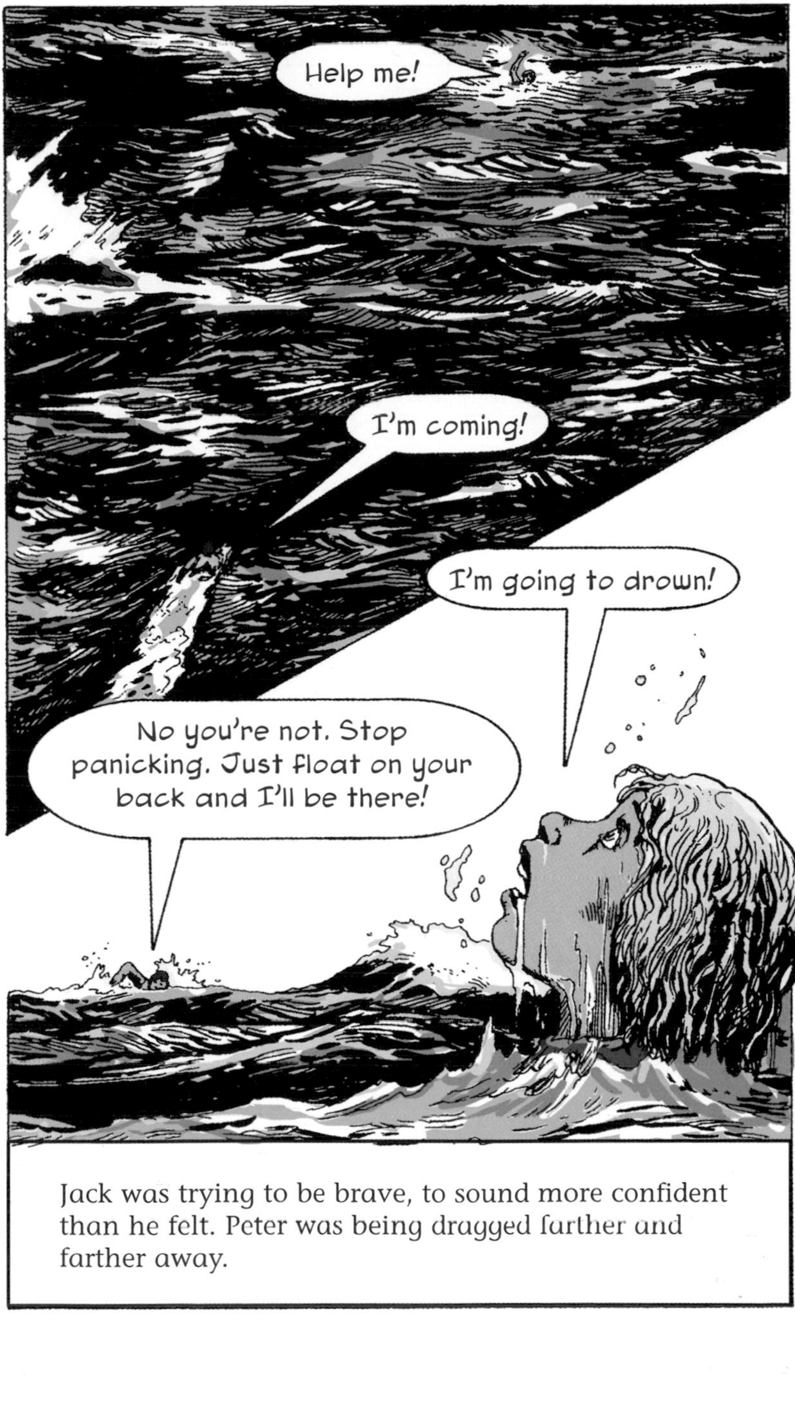
Help me!
I'm coming!
I'm going to drown!
No you're not. Stop panicking. Just float on your back and I'll be there!

Jack was trying to be brave, to sound more confident than he felt. Peter was being dragged farther and farther away.

Suddenly, the waves around Jack shined like gold. Spray leapt into the air and began to make a human shape. It hung just above the surface of the sea.

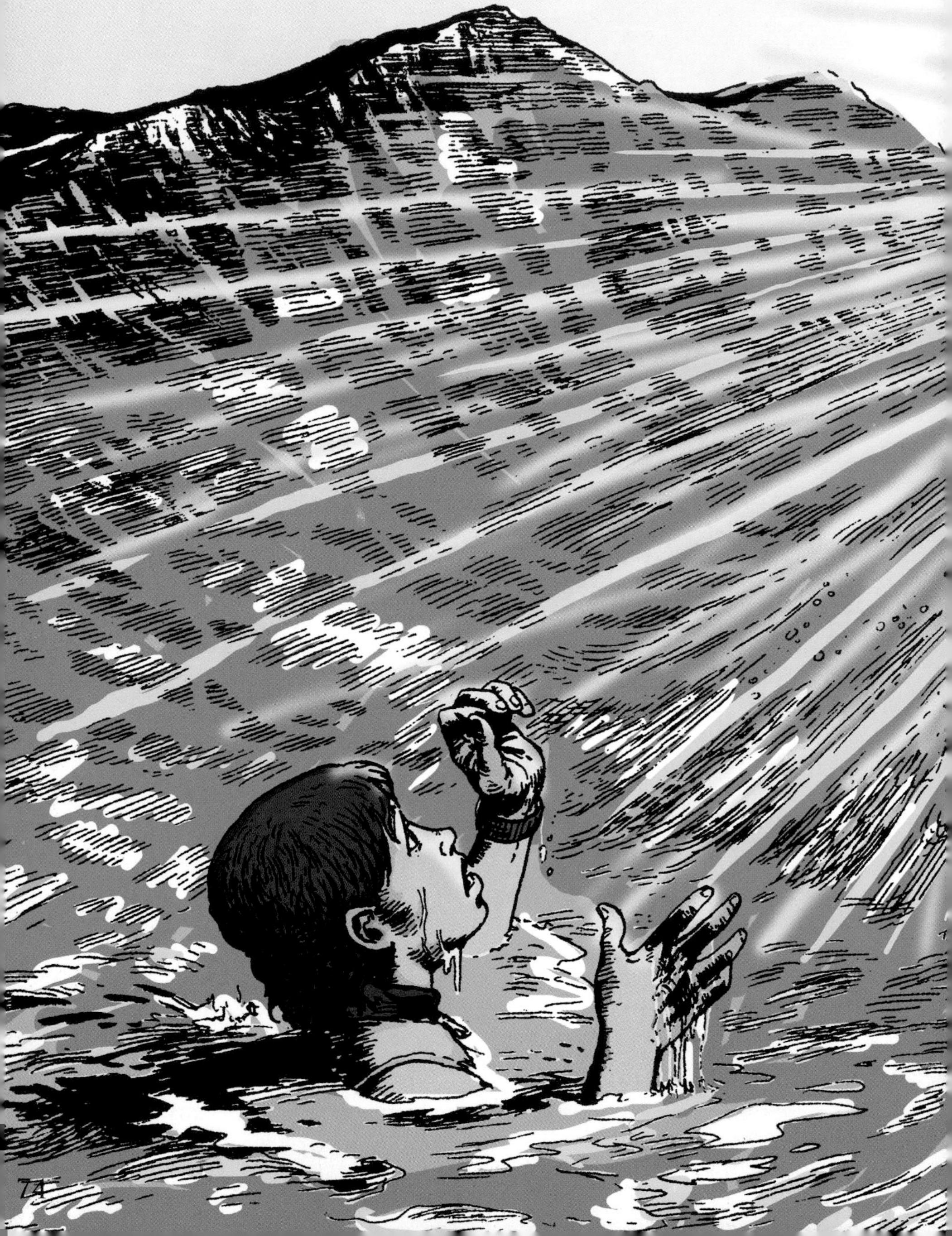

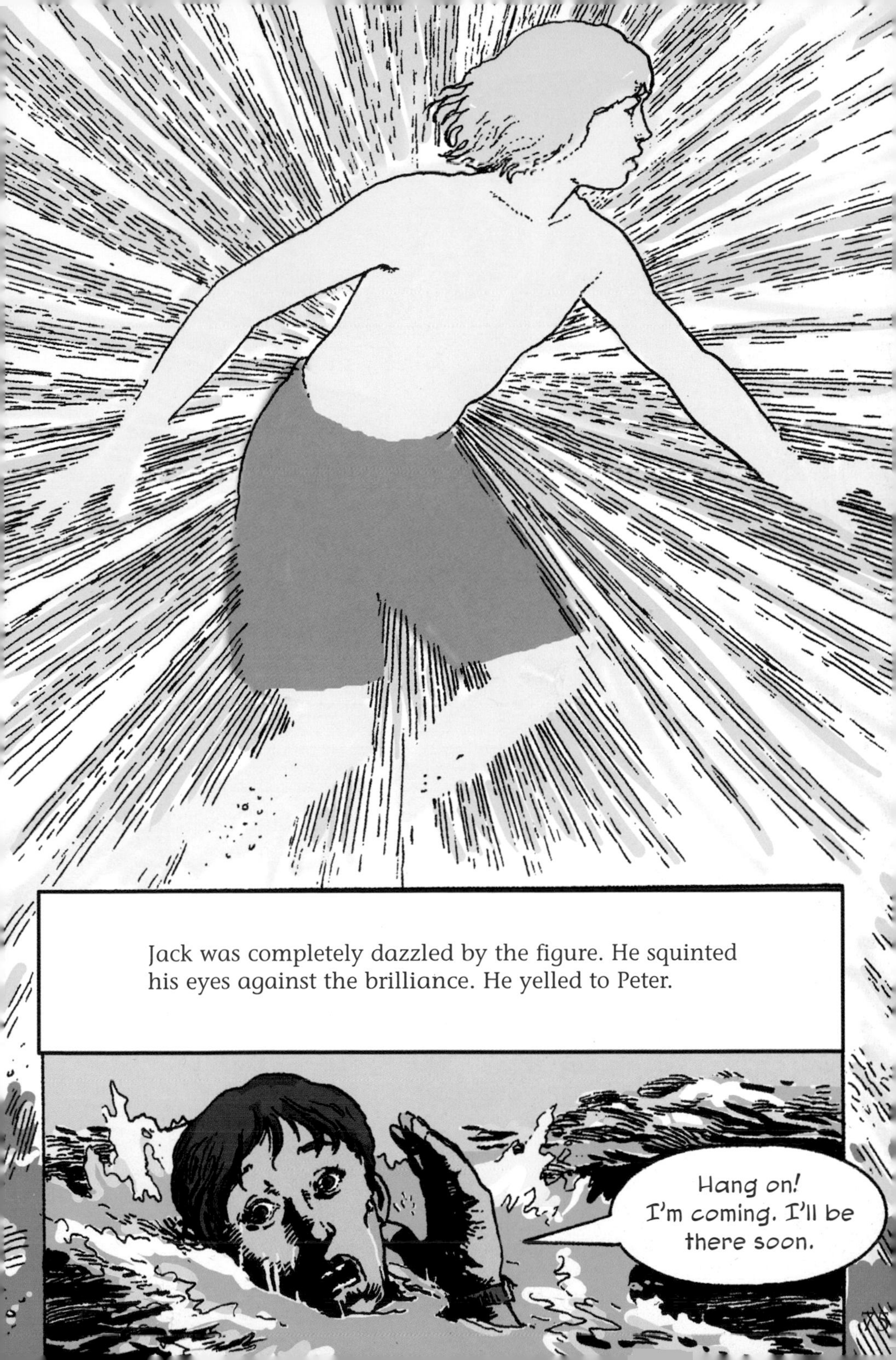
Jack was completely dazzled by the figure. He squinted his eyes against the brilliance. He yelled to Peter.
Hang on! I'm coming. I'll be there soon.

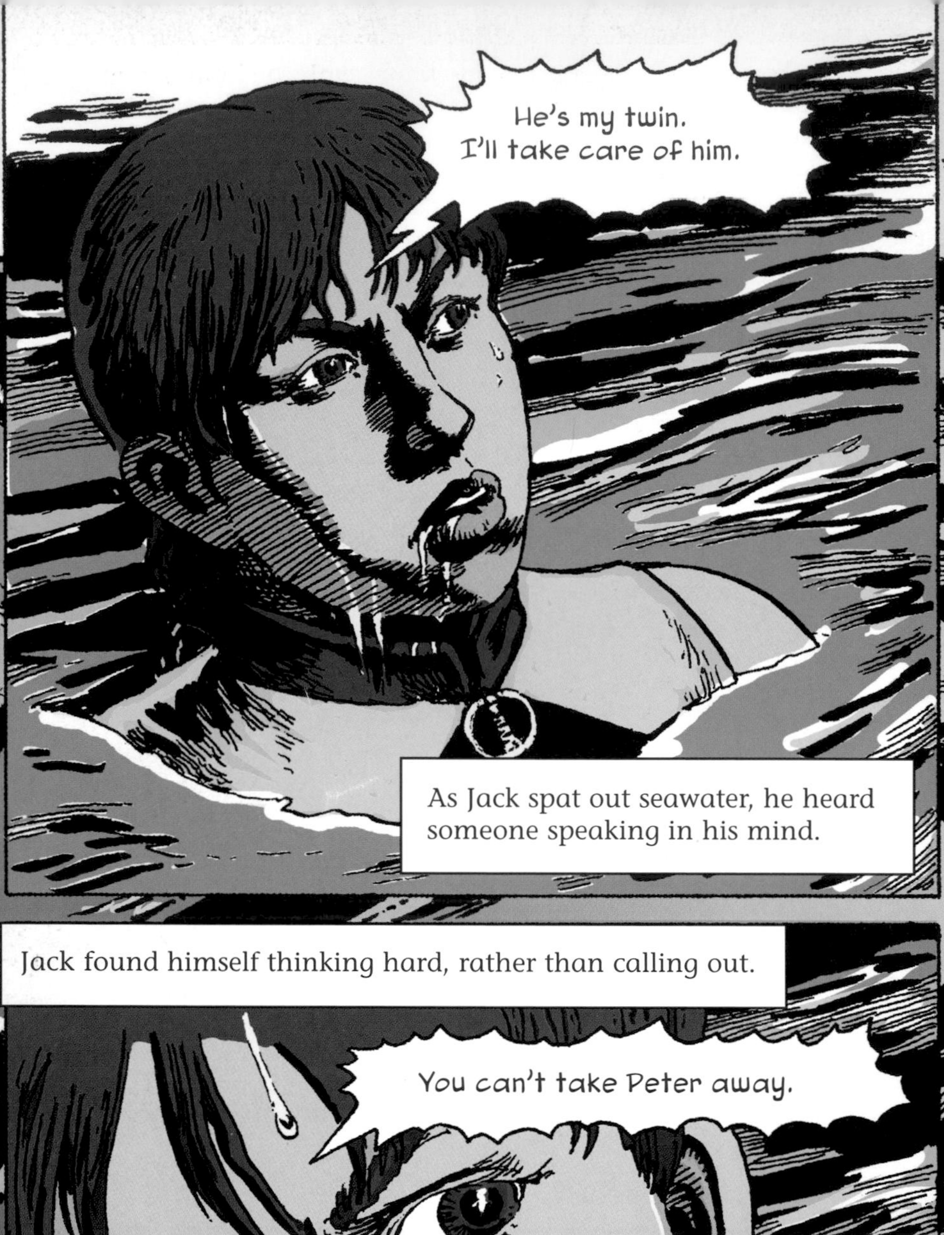
He's my twin.
I'll take care of him.
As Jack spat out seawater, he heard someone speaking in his mind.
Jack found himself thinking hard, rather than calling out.
You can't take Peter away.

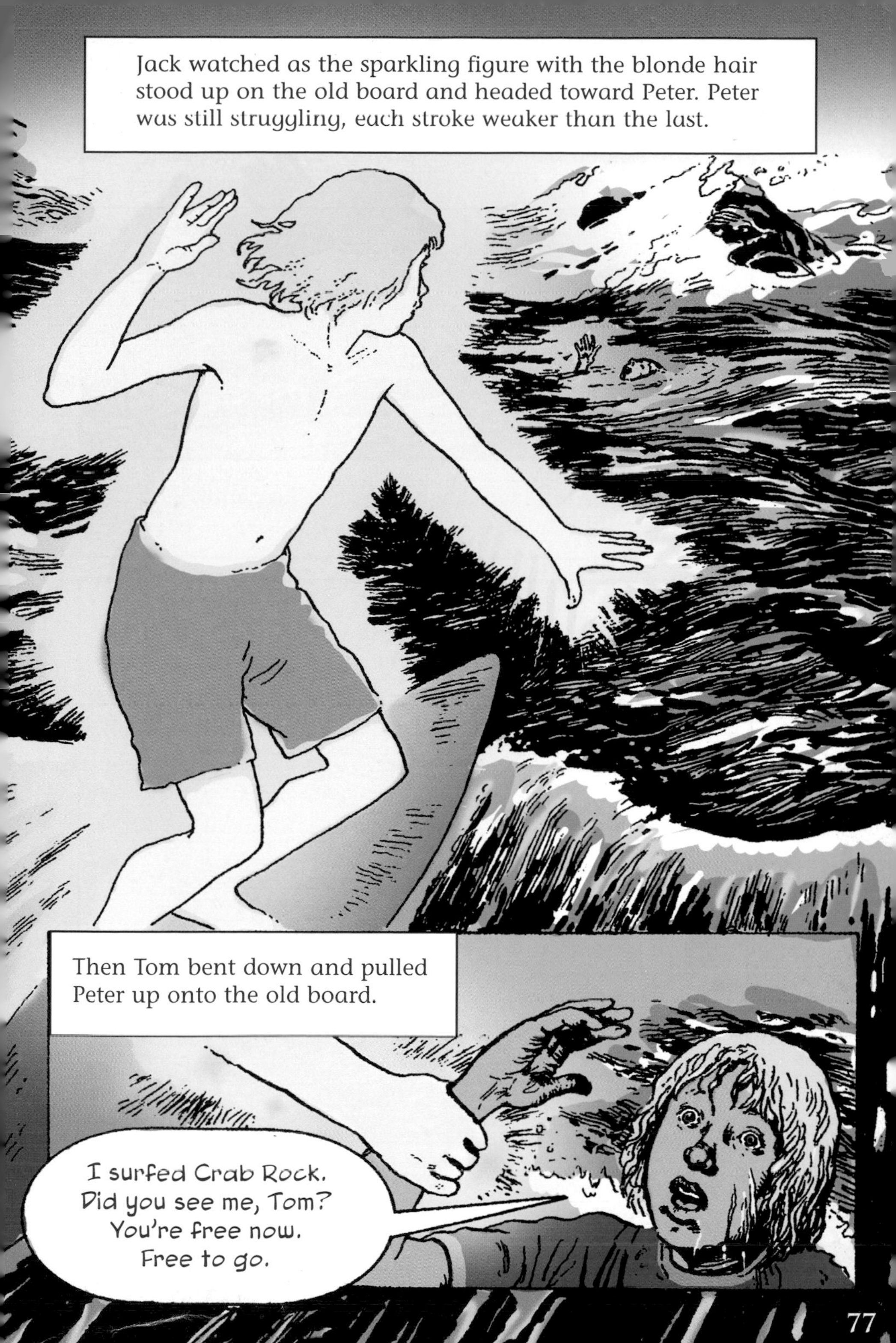
Jack watched as the sparkling figure with the blonde hair stood up on the old board and headed toward Peter. Peter was still struggling, each stroke weaker than the last.
Then Tom bent down and pulled Peter up onto the old board.
I surfed Crab Rock. Did you see me, Tom? You're free now. Free to go.

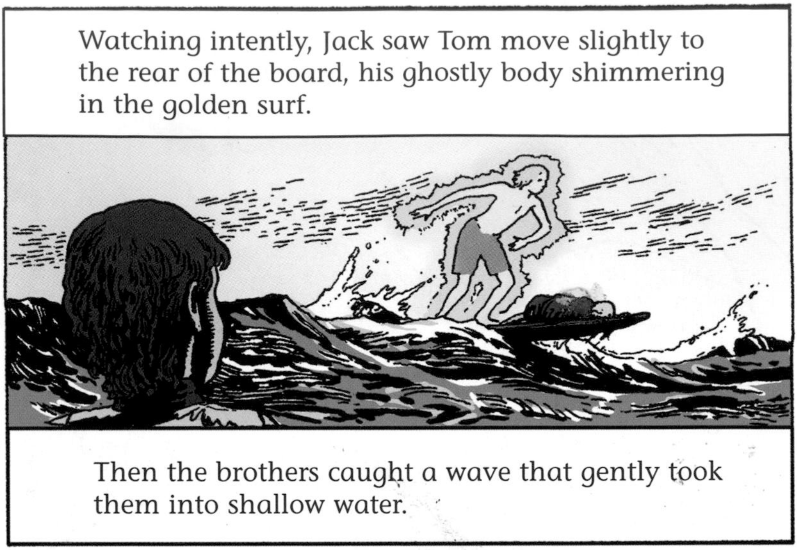
Watching intently, Jack saw Tom move slightly to the rear of the board, his ghostly body shimmering in the golden surf.
Then the brothers caught a wave that gently took them into shallow water.

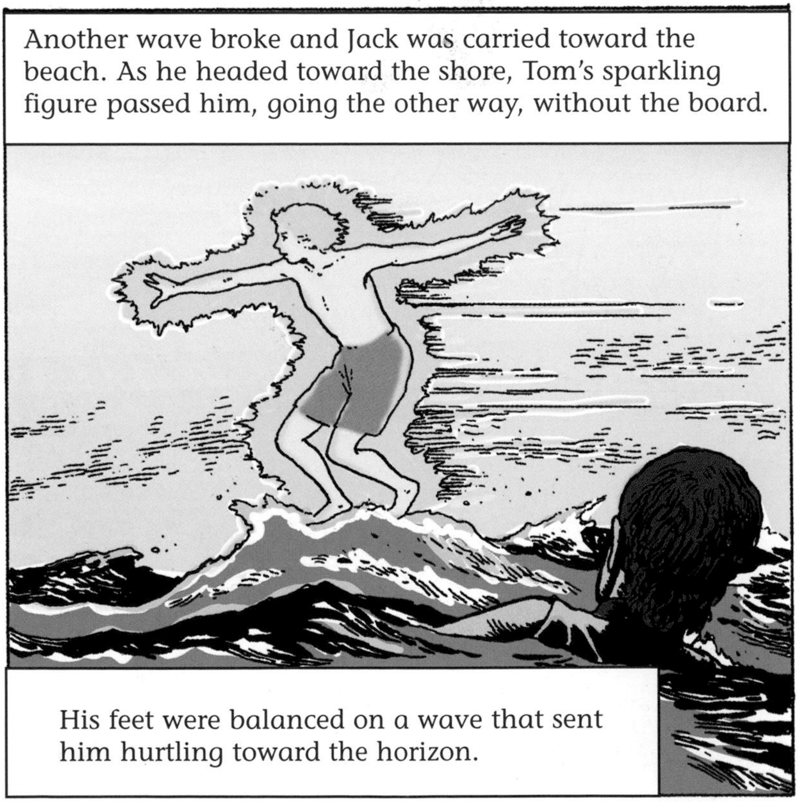
Another wave broke and Jack was carried toward the beach. As he headed toward the shore, Tom's sparkling figure passed him, going the other way, without the board.
His feet were balanced on a wave that sent him hurtling toward the horizon.

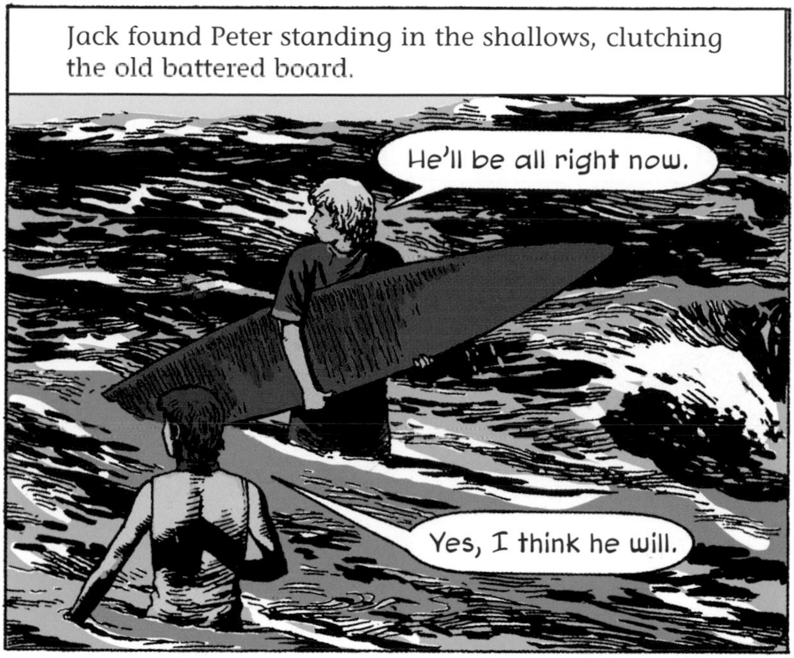
Jack found Peter standing in the shallows, clutching the old battered board.
He'll be all right now.
Yes, I think he will.

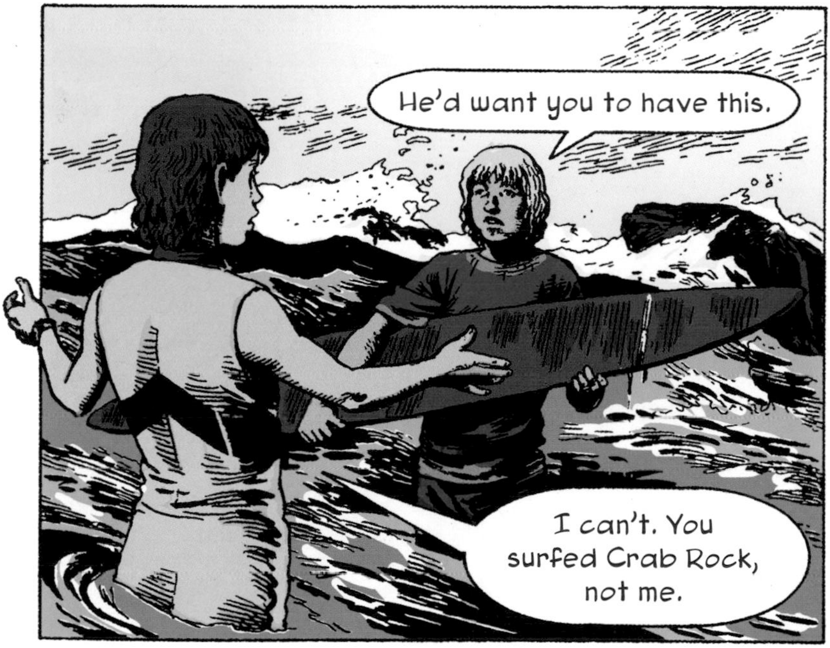
He'd want you to have this.
I can't. You surfed Crab Rock, not me.

But Peter insisted.

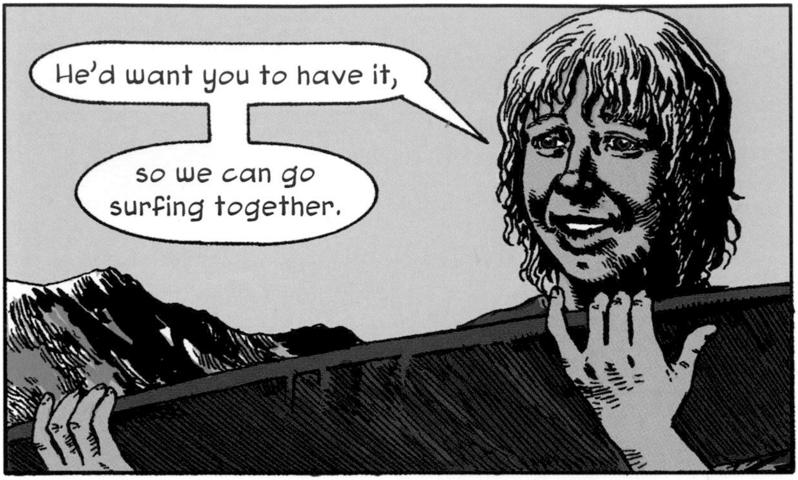
He'd want you to have it,
so we can go surfing together.

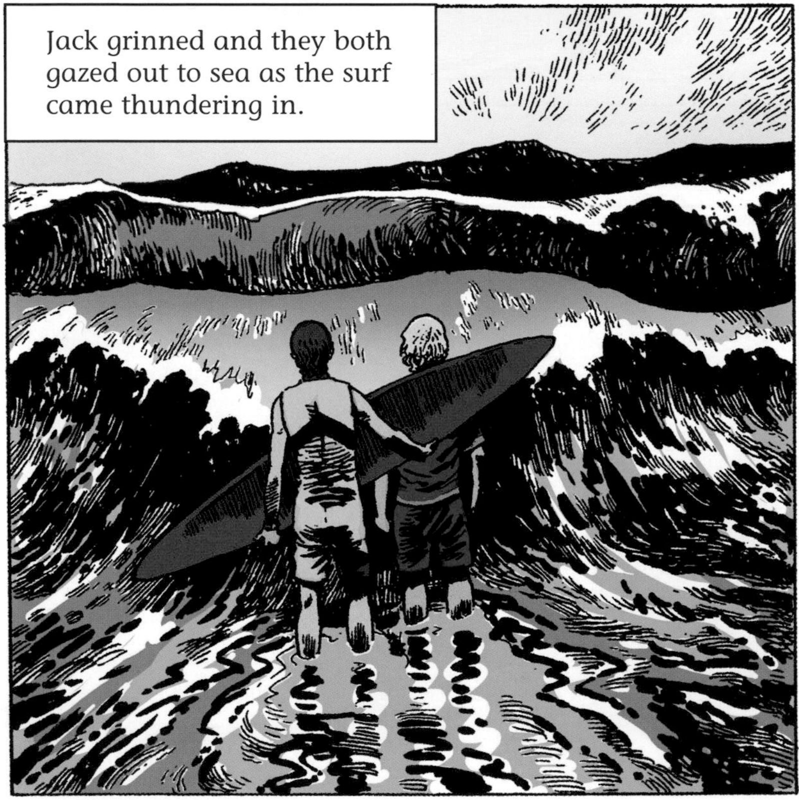
Jack grinned and they both gazed out to sea as the surf came thundering in.

ABOUT THE AUTHOR

Anthony Masters published his first book when he was 24. For the rest of his life, he wrote fiction and nonfiction for children and adults, winning awards along the way. *Junior Booklist* magazine once wrote that Masters knew how to "pack a story full of fast-moving incidents." Masters himself once said he would like to be a fox, because the creature is so cunning. Anthony Masters died in 2003.

ABOUT THE ILLUSTRATOR

Peter Dennis has illustrated hundreds of books. His largest project was illustrating the entire bible! When he is not working, Dennis likes to collect toy soldiers and ride motorbikes. His favorite artist is the American Howard Pyle who illustrated stories about Robin Hood. Dennis lives in Nottinghamshire in England, which is where Robin Hood once lived, robbing from the rich and giving to the poor.

GLOSSARY

aggressive (uh-GRESS-iv)—quick to attack or start a fight

barnacles (BAR-nuh-kuhlz)—ocean creatures that form a hard shell and attach themselves to underwater surfaces such as rocks

breakers (BRAY-kurz)—waves that break into foam when they reach shore

crest (KREST)—the top of a wave

feeble (FEE-buhl)—lacking strength; weak

humiliated (hyoo-MIL-ee-ate-id)—to lower the self-respect or pride of someone

reef (REEF)—a strip of rock, sand, or coral near the surface of a body of water

reluctantly (ri-LUHK-tuhnt-lee)—not willingly

submerged (suhb-MERJD)—sunk under the surface of water

undertow (UHN-dur-toh)—a current below the surface that pulls away from the shore

INTERNET SITES

Do you want to know more about subjects related to this book? Or are you interested in learning about other topics? Then check out FactHound, a fun, easy way to find Internet sites.

Our investigative staff has already sniffed out great sites for you!

Here's how to use FactHound:

1. Visit *www.facthound.com*

2. Select your grade level.

3. To learn more about subjects related to this book, type in the book's ISBN number: **1598890808**.

4. Click the **Fetch It** button.

FactHound will fetch the best Internet sites for you.

DISCUSSION QUESTIONS

1. Do you believe in ghosts? Talk about it and explain your thinking.

2. Why did Jack risk going after the surfboard in the dangerous storm? What do you think of his decision? What might he have done differently? Explain your answers.

3. On page 30, why does Peter seem afraid when he meets Jack?

4. Jack and Peter talked about "spirits resting in peace." What does this mean to you? Does it make sense? Why or why not?

WRITING PROMPTS

1. On page 7, Jack says that "everyone here is soft. I used to be a hard guy back home." What does he mean by this? Is he a hard or soft character by the end of the story? Write about his character.

2. How do you feel about protecting your friends? When do you get involved and when do you not? Write a story where you and your friends get into a dangerous adventure at the beach. How do you rescue them?

3. Write about another possible title for this story. Explain why you think your choice is better (or scarier or more exciting) than "Haunted Surfboard."

ALSO PUBLISHED BY STONE ARCH BOOKS

ABRACADABRA
BY ALEX GUTTERIDGE
BECCA HAS A GHOSTLY DOUBLE!
STONE ARCH Graphic Novel

Abracadabra
by Alex Gutteridge

Tom is about to come face-to-face with Charlotte, Becca's double. But there's something strange about this, because Charlotte died three hundred and fifty years ago.

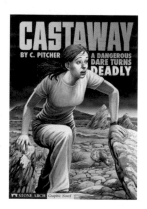

CASTAWAY
BY C. PITCHER
A DANGEROUS DARE TURNS DEADLY
STONE ARCH Graphic Novel

Castaway
by C. Pitcher

Six kids on a geography trip are cut off by the sea. One of them is hurt, it's the middle of the night, and they have only themselves to blame.